DEAR DIARY, WHERE ARE YOU?

Slowly I focused on the inside of my locker. Something was wrong. It was a mess. A total mess! I looked around helplessly at all the other kids scrambling through the things in their lockers and pitching them onto the floor. Somebody must have sneaked in and switched everything around.

"Oh, NO!" I shrieked as I remembered what I had left in my locker the day before. I had to get it back if it was the last thing I ever did.

Suddenly I saw something straight ahead of me that made my heart stop, and the rest of me stopped, too. Jana Morgan and her friends were standing in a tight little cluster looking at something that Jana was holding. They were giggling and talking excitedly. I knew without looking. They had found the last thing in the world I wanted them to see—*my secret, personal diary!*

THE TRUTH ABOUT TAFFY SINCLAIR

Betsy Haynes

A BANTAM SKYLARK BOOK®
TORONTO · NEW YORK · LONDON · SYDNEY · AUCKLAND

RL 5, 009-012

THE TRUTH ABOUT TAFFY SINCLAIR
A Bantam Skylark Book / July 1988

*Skylark Books is a registered trademark of Bantam Books, a division of
Bantam Doubleday Dell Publishing Group, Inc.
Registered in U.S. Patent and Trademark Office and elsewhere.*

ISBN 0-553-15607-1

Published simultaneously in the United States and Canada

*Bantam Books are published by Bantam Books, a division of Bantam
Doubleday Dell Publishing Group, Inc. Its trademark, consisting of the
words "Bantam Books" and the portrayal of a rooster, is Registered in
U.S. Patent and Trademark Office and in other countries. Marca
Registrada. Bantam Books, 666 Fifth Avenue, New York, New York 10103.*

PRINTED IN THE UNITED STATES OF AMERICA

S   0 9 8 7 6 5 4 3 2 1

1 *

"Come on, Taffy. Get moving! It's almost time to leave for school and you haven't done your exercises yet. How do you ever expect to become a fashion model if you don't keep your figure trim?"

"Coming, Mother." I groaned as I hurried down the stairs from my bedroom. Can't she ever let up? I thought. She was sitting at the kitchen table in her bathrobe with her blond hair still in rollers. It was hard to believe she still wore rollers. They went out with the hula hoop.

"Don't forget your ballet lesson after school," she went on, "and that reminds me." Her coffee cup stopped in midair, and her face brightened. "I just

1

heard about a wonderful diction coach in New Haven. I'm going to call her today and see if she can take you as a student over the summer. Then when we line up some television commercials for you, you'll be able to do your own speaking parts instead of letting someone else do the voice-overs. In fact, I'll bet we'll be able to get you some jobs doing voice-overs for other girls. It's going to be thrilling for you to be in show business, honey." She paused and gazed off into the distance. "Just as it was for me when I was one of the Radio City Music Hall Rockettes."

My mother was still talking as I raced past her into the family room and hurried through my exercises. Fashion model. Television commercials. Voice-overs. Radio City Rockettes. That was all she ever thought about.

Not me. I had *plenty* of other things to think about, especially since this was the last week of classes before the summer. I finished my exercises, grabbed my books, and headed for school. I was finally leaving grade school behind and going into junior high, I thought with satisfaction. No more Mark Twain Elementary. No more Jana Morgan and her snobby friends and their big deal club, The Fabulous Five.

The thought of Jana made me bristle. Ever since I could remember she and her friends, Beth Barry, Melanie Edwards, Christie Winchell, and Katie Shannon, had caused me one problem after another, but Jana was definitely the worst. In fifth grade she started a club against me called The Against Taffy Sinclair Club, but this year in sixth grade it was the absolute pits. She *still* tried to turn everybody against me, including Randy Kirwan, the boy I like. Not only that, The Fabulous Five were all jealous of me because of my looks. Can I help it if I have naturally blond hair and blue eyes? They are also jealous because I had a part in a daytime drama called *Interns and Lovers* that was on network television last fall and was seen by millions of people all across America, and now I was going to get modeling jobs, first here in Bridgeport, Connecticut, but later on probably even in New York City. I guess I could understand why they were all jealous of me. But still, Jana was my number one enemy, with each of her friends tying for second place.

But what did they know, anyway? They certainly didn't know as much about me as they thought they did. And they never would, either. I'd see to that.

"Ha!" I said out loud. "They think they're so smart when really they're just a bunch of immature babies." Thank goodness there would be lots of new kids at Wakeman Junior High this fall. I wouldn't have to be bothered with Jana or the others anymore. I sighed. This was Tuesday, and school would be out on Friday. Just four more days to go.

Alexis Duvall ran up to me the instant I stepped onto the school ground. "Hi, Taffy. Did you hear the news? Clarence Marshall doesn't think he's going to pass. Wouldn't that be gross? Being left behind in grade school while everyone else goes on to junior high?"

"It would serve him right for being such a jerk," I said, remembering how he had tried to plaster one of his slobbery kisses on me at Kim Baxter's pool party last summer.

"I know, but wouldn't it be *gross*?" she insisted. Then she looked toward the school building and added under her breath, "Shark alert. Shark alert. Here comes Curtis Trowbridge and I think he's heading for us."

"Oh, no," I groaned. Curtis Trowbridge was the nerdiest person alive and being seen talking to him was totally embarrassing. But here he came anyway, straight toward us. He was walking along with his glasses bouncing on his nose and a pencil stuck behind his left ear, and he was concentrating on the notepad he always carried when he did interviews for the *Mark Twain Sentinel*. Curtis was sixth-grade editor of the paper.

"Hi, girls," said Curtis in a crackling voice. "You're two of the people I want to see."

"Great," Alexis muttered, but Curtis didn't seem to hear.

"I'm having a graduation party at my house Friday night, and you're both invited."

Alexis and I exchanged wide-eyed looks of horror. A graduation party? At Curtis Trowbridge's house? I couldn't think of anything worse.

"I don't know if I can make it," I said, feeling suddenly grateful to my mother. "I may have to audition for a part in a television commercial."

"Gee, Taffy. That's too bad," said Curtis. He looked genuinely sorry. "Everybody else who I've talked to is coming. How about you, Alexis?"

Alexis shrugged. "Well . . ." she stammered. "If everybody else is coming . . ."

"Great!" cried Curtis. "I'll put you down as a 'yes'." He made some marks in his notepad, pushed up his glasses with a finger, and then turned around and went zipping off in the direction of Lisa Snow and Kim Baxter, who were standing by the swings.

"Do you really think everyone will be there?" I asked Alexis.

"They had better be," she said with a frown.

I tried to act casual as I sauntered up the sidewalk with Alexis, but secretly I was looking around for Randy Kirwan. He would be easy to spot since he was the handsomest boy in Mark Twain Elementary, with dark, wavy hair and big blue eyes. I had to find out if he was going to Curtis's party. There was no way to know how often I would see him over the summer, if I would even see him at all. So if he was going to the party, I had to go, too. It might be my last chance for a long time to take him away from Jana Morgan.

Before I could spot Randy anywhere on the playground, the first bell rang. "Rats!" I mumbled under my breath and headed for my locker. Maybe I would get the chance to talk to him at recess.

There was absolute pandemonium in the hall where the sixth-grade lockers stood. Kids were jerking their locker doors open and shrieking to each other. I tried to ignore the chaos as I headed for my own locker. It's just end of the year hysteria, I thought with disgust. You wouldn't catch me acting so juvenile.

Yesterday Miss Wiggins, our sixth-grade teacher, had collected all the locks and instructed us to bring paper bags to school today. We were supposed to clean out our lockers and take home everything we wouldn't need for the last few days of class. I sighed as I pulled my locker door open. I had forgotten my bag, and I had a ton of things to take home. Things I didn't especially want anyone else to see. I certainly didn't want to stack them on my desk and take the chance of somebody's poking through them when I wasn't looking. Maybe I would call Mother and ask her to drop off a grocery bag for me.

Slowly I focused on the inside of my locker. Something was wrong. It was a mess. A total mess! I never left my things like that. I always kept my locker neat. I bent down, grabbing books and papers from out of the jumble. "These aren't mine," I whispered incredulously.

There were drawings of tanks and airplanes. A math book with Matt Zeboski's name in it. Marcie Bee's spelling paper with the one and only A she had ever gotten in spelling on it. It was the paper she kept taped inside *her* locker door.

I looked around helplessly at all the other kids scrambling through the things in their lockers and pitching them onto the floor. Suddenly I understood what was going on. It wasn't end of the year hysteria, after all. Nobody had their own things! Somebody must have sneaked in after the locks were turned in to Miss Wiggins and switched everything around. And in the center of the hall Keith Masterson, Richie Corrierro, and Joel Murphy were doubled over with fits of laughter.

"OH, NO!" I shrieked as I remembered what I had left in my locker the day before. "Who has it?" I cried, but nobody could hear me over the noise. I stomped up the hall, jerking my head first to the right and then to the left. I had to find it. I had to get it back if it was the last thing I ever did.

Suddenly I saw something straight ahead of me that made my heart stop, and then the rest of me stopped, too. Jana Morgan and her friends were standing in a tight little cluster looking at something that Jana was holding in her hand. They were giggling and talking excitedly. I couldn't see what it was that Jana had because the others were standing too close to her for me to get a good view. But I knew. I knew without looking. They had found the last thing in the world I wanted them to see—*my secret, personal diary.*

2 ❋

Miss Wiggins came steaming up the hall like a battleship with her red corkscrew curls sticking out in all directions like warning flags.

"What is going on here?" she demanded as she came to a halt. "Kim Baxter has just informed me that *someone* has invaded the lockers and switched all the contents around."

Keith, Joel, and Richie magically faded from the center of the hallway. Seconds later their faces, looking properly solemn and concerned, reappeared between the heads of other sixth-graders.

"That's right, Miss Wiggins," Joel said with amazing innocence. "Things are a real mess."

"You can say that again," shouted Katie Shannon. "Nobody has any business getting into our lockers and messing with our private property."

"Somebody took my new pink sweater," complained Lisa Snow. "I just got it for my birthday last week."

"My Billy Joel poster is gone, too," added Kim Baxter. "I'll *die* if anything happens to it."

All through the hall kids were grumbling about things that were missing from their lockers. I thought about going straight to Miss Wiggins and telling her about my diary and about Jana and her friends having it. It would serve them right to get in trouble for not giving it back immediately! Even though my name wasn't on it, I could identify it easily. The cover was softly padded with fabric that was the same shade of blue as my eyes, and there was a strap made out of the blue fabric that reached around from the back cover and slipped into the lock on the front.

Still, I thought, there's a million-to-one chance that what they were looking at *wasn't* my diary. In that case, someone else might have it and not realize what they had. It was locked, of course, and I had the key in my purse. And it didn't have my name on the outside. But at the same time, it was pretty obvious that it was a diary, and a lot of kids would give nearly anything to get their hands on it if they knew it was mine. Besides that, there were things written in it that no one on the face of this earth should ever see, I thought with a shiver. I didn't dare call attention to the fact that my diary was missing. Whoever had it would be certain to break it open and read it.

"I want to know this instant who is responsible," said Miss Wiggins.

Nearly twenty pairs of eyes zeroed in on Keith and Joel and Richie.

"We didn't do it," insisted Keith, throwing up his arms in a giant shrug.

"Who are you trying to kid, Masterson?" said Katie Shannon. She took a menacing step toward the boys. "You guys were really breaking up when the rest of us opened our lockers and saw what had happened."

"So?" said Richie, thrusting his face forward so that his nose almost touched Katie's. "Since when is it a crime to laugh? We got here first, that's all."

"Yeah," said Joel. "You should have seen how all of you looked. It was a riot."

Miss Wiggins frowned thoughtfully at the boys. "All right, boys and girls. That's enough," she said. "We'll settle this later. Right now, I want you to go through the contents of your lockers and return everything you can to its proper owner. Bring whatever you have left over to the classroom."

The instant Miss Wiggins was gone, pandemonium broke out again as kids began digging through the messes in their lockers and pitching things through the air to each other. I stared into my locker for a moment, ducking once as a lavender sneaker whizzed past my ear, but I didn't touch anything. I had something else to do first. Something that was much more important than returning Matt Zeboski's math book or Marcie Bee's spelling paper.

I whirled around and marched straight to Jana Morgan's locker. "I think you have something of mine, and I want it back right now!" I demanded.

Jana looked at me, first with surprise and then with disgust. "I don't have anything of yours. If I did, I'd give it to you."

Jana's friends gathered around us. "What do you think we have?" asked Christie. "Something important?"

"I know you have it," I insisted. "I saw you all bunched up and giggling over something one of you had found. You can't fool me."

"Did it have your name on it?" asked Melanie with a sly smile.

I glared at her without answering.

"Because if it did," Melanie went on, "you'll get it back. Wiggins said we had to give everything back that we could identify."

"Then give it back to me now," I challenged. There was still the nagging thought that they might not have it, but I couldn't back down.

"What we were giggling over was a dirty magazine," said Christie in an exasperated voice. "We *thought* it belonged to one of the boys. Gosh, Taffy! Was it yours?"

With that, they all started laughing like crazy. Just as my face started turning red at the insinuation that the dirty magazine belonged to me, I felt someone tap me on the shoulder. "Taffy, does this belong to you?"

It was Randy's voice. I fought down the blush and turned toward him, opening my eyes wide and giving him my best smile. I couldn't believe my good luck.

Randy was holding out a social studies book and smiling back at me. He had such a gorgeous smile that my knees got weak. Jana must be just about to die, I thought. What does he see in her anyway?

"Let me look at it," I said. Then I moved away from the girls so that Randy would have to turn his back on them and follow me.

My heart was pounding as I took the book out of his hand and pretended to look at it. I wanted him to like me so much! Here was my chance to talk to him and maybe make a good impression. I smiled at him again and tossed my head so that my long blond hair would fall over one shoulder. I had seen a beautiful girl in a movie do that once, and the guy who was watching fell madly in love with her in that very scene.

My name was right inside the front cover of the social studies book, so I couldn't stall any longer. "Thanks," I said as sweetly as I could. "I REALLY appreciate it."

"Sure," he said. Then he turned back to his own locker and started rummaging through it again.

I tossed a triumphant look toward Jana and her friends, who were pretending not to notice that I had been talking to Randy, and went back to my locker. They could pretend all they wanted, I thought with satisfaction, but Randy had been talking to *me* instead of Jana, and they knew it. Then suddenly it dawned on me. I had the perfect chance to ask him about Curtis's party, and I blew it. Of course I knew whose fault it was, I thought angrily. Jana's and her snobby friends'. How could I possibly think straight when they had my diary?

The final bell had already rung by the time we finished giving back possessions, and the last of our class trooped through the hall carrying the odds and ends we still couldn't identify. Someone's high-topped gym shoe. An open bag of potato chips. Things like that. A couple of teachers peered out of their rooms to see what all the commotion was about, and Mr. Mullins shushed us, making more noise himself than we were making.

Miss Wiggins was waiting for us inside the classroom door, directing us to put our leftovers, as she called them, on the table in the reading corner at the back of the room. I dumped a pair of wrinkled boy's gym shorts and an overdue library book onto the table, hoping to see my diary, but it wasn't there. At least not so far. Other kids were still straggling into the room, including Jana and Melanie. They had to put my diary on that table. *They just had to.*

"All right, boys and girls," Miss Wiggins called out when everyone had finally settled into their desks.

"Now you may go back to the table and claim what's yours. We'll go by *rows*!" she cautioned, as Mark Peters bolted from his seat. Pointing her finger as if she were controlling a puppet, she directed him back into a sitting position. "Now," she said in a calmer voice. "Row one. You may go."

I kept on craning my neck to try to see if my diary was lying on the table. I couldn't. But by the time Miss Wiggins called the fourth row, which is mine *and* Jana Morgan's, there was hardly anything left. I shoved aside a brown banana, a spiral notebook with all the sheets torn out, and at least four more library books, hoping to uncover the book I was looking for.

Then I saw something. Something at the bottom of the pile. My heart skipped a beat. It wasn't my diary. It wasn't even blue. What I had found was a dirty magazine.

3 ✻

"**B**ack to your seats, please," Miss Wiggins commanded as three kids from the last row of desks lingered over the table, poking through the odds and ends from the lockers. "You'll have other chances to look the things over during both recesses and lunch period."

Sinking a little lower in my seat, I tried to concentrate as she started the math lesson, but my mind was still on my diary. Since no one had given it to me or put it on the table with the other leftovers, that could only mean one thing. It was pretty obvious that whoever had it realized what they had found. They knew it was a diary, and what was worse, they

18

undoubtedly knew that it was mine. Who could possibly care what any of the other girls in this class would write in a diary? They were all too immature to have anything interesting going on in their lives as I do. Not one of them had ever been on television. And even though Jana and her snobby friends had been in the same modeling class with me, not one of them could ever get a job as a model. That was why the person—or *people*—who found my diary were keeping it. They were planning to break it open and read it and try to find out all my secrets. Of course, I had written other things, too.

I glanced over my shoulder at Jana Morgan. She was following the math lesson in her book. I cringed as I imagined her reading all the things I had written about her and the other members of The Fabulous Five. In my mind I could see them holding a meeting of their club in Jana's bedroom and huddling together to read my diary. Or maybe they would pass it around and take turns reading it out loud.

Dear Diary:

Jana Morgan is my worst enemy in the world. What I can't understand is why she is so popular. She isn't pretty at all! She has a rotten personality. And she's never done anything special such as being on TV the way I have. She probably bribes people to be her friends!

Dear Diary:

Today Beth Barry looked like a clown. She's always acting dramatic and theatrical and trying to show off by wearing loud clothes, but today was the worst. She had on a fuchsia outfit that made me want to throw up!

She thinks she's going to be a great actress some day, but I'm the one who has already had an acting role on TV. Ha!!

Dear Diary:

Christie Winchell is so boring that she wouldn't have any friends if her mother weren't principal of the school and people didn't want to butter her up. I mean, let's face it. She's such a math genius that all she thinks about are numbers and equations. How much fun is it to be friends with a computer?

Dear Diary:

Today I saw Christie Winchell flirting with Mr. Scott, the assistant principal. She thinks nobody notices that she has a humongous crush on him, but everybody does. She's so obvious about it that I'll bet even Mr. Scott notices and is laughing at her behind her back.

Dear Diary:

Katie Shannon acts so disgusting. She is always saying that being pretty isn't important and that she can't stand boys. How could anyone be so dumb!?!

Dear Diary:

Melanie Edwards should go on a diet! She has started to lose weight and looks a lot better than she did when she stuffed herself with brownies all the time, but she still has a long way to go.

In my imagination I could see all of their faces turn purple with rage as they read what I had said about them.

"Who does she think she is to write stuff like that?" Beth would probably yell, and everybody else would nod, except for Christie, who would curl up in a corner of Jana's bedroom wondering how she would ever face Mr. Scott again and wishing that she were dead.

Well, the truth hurts! I thought contemptuously. I was remembering all the times those five had done mean things to me. There was the time in fifth grade when I got a card in the mail that said "You must have been a beautiful baby, but baby, look at you now" on the front, and had a picture of King Kong on the inside. Nobody had signed it, but I knew it was from them.

But then I remembered the dirty magazine left on the table. Wasn't that what Christie had said they were looking at when I thought they were giggling over my diary? What if they didn't have it, after all? Then, who did?

Randy? I thought with a panic. *Could Randy Kirwan possibly have it?* Of course, he was too polite to break it open and read what I had written about *him*. But what if he forgot to put it on the table with the other things people couldn't identify? And what if he remembered it after he got home? And he had it with him? And he broke it open? Just so he could find out whom it belonged to, of course. And what if he read what I had written about him? On practically every page.

Dear Diary:
I am so much in love with Randy Kirwan that I can hardly stand it.
Today I . . .

"Taffy Sinclair!"

Miss Wiggins's voice cut through my nightmare. "I know that this is the last week of school and that everybody is having a hard time keeping his mind on the work. But would it be too much trouble to ask you to join our social studies lesson this morning?"

I blinked. Social studies lesson? What had happened to math? I locked my jaws to keep my mouth from quivering and tried to smile at her. I would die if anyone guessed how embarrassed I was.

"Sorry, Miss Wiggins," I mumbled as I shoved my math book into my desk and pulled out my social studies book.

Just then I heard Jana Morgan clear her throat. I stiffened like a poker and listened. I knew what was coming next, and I was right. An instant later Melanie Edwards cleared her throat. Then one by one, Beth Barry, Christie Winchell, and Katie Shannon all cleared their throats, too.

It was a signal. It had to be. It meant that they knew how embarrassed I was, and they were glad. Not only that, they were out to get me. I had to get that diary back if it was the last thing I ever did.

4 ✳

At morning recess everybody was talking about the big locker disaster. Everybody, that is, except Jana and her friends. As usual, they were standing by the fence acting as if they were too good to associate with anyone else.

"Can you believe the nerve of those three boys?" Lisa Snow was saying to a group of girls as I walked up. "Sneaking back into the school like that and messing up the lockers."

"I ought to make them pay for my Billy Joel poster," complained Kim Baxter.

"Didn't you get it back?" asked Sara Sawyer.

"Yes, but one corner was torn off!"

"Did everybody get all their things back?" I asked as casually as I could.

"Sure," said Lisa. "Is something of yours still missing?"

I didn't answer for a moment. I knew that any of them might have my diary. Just because they acted friendly sometimes didn't mean that they wouldn't love to get their hands on it if they could. "I'm not sure," I said, deciding not to take any chances. "I can't remember if I left something in my locker last night or if I took it home."

A couple of girls shrugged, but no one mentioned finding anything that might be mine. Then Sara started talking about Curtis Trowbridge's party.

"I wonder what a party at Curtis's house will be like, anyway?"

Kim made a face. "He's such a nerd. You don't suppose we'll have to work crossword puzzles or play games on his computer, do you?"

Everybody laughed at that.

"I guess we'll find out Friday night," said Lisa. "Everybody is going."

I took a deep breath to keep my heart from pounding. No one had said anything about boys, but if *everyone* was going, that had to mean them, including Randy Kirwan. I was trying to think of a way to bring up Randy's name without being too obvious when someone tapped me on the shoulder.

"Hi, Taffy. Are you going to Curtis's party?"

"Oh, hi, Mona," I said. I knew she would be able to hear the disappointment in my voice, but I couldn't help it. Mona Vaughn was nice and everything, but she was really the pits when it came to looks, even now that Jana and her friends had given her a new hairstyle. She still didn't know how to dress or walk across the room like a model or any of the *important* things. Even her hair didn't look that great. To make matters worse, she followed me around most of the time. It was embarrassing to be seen with someone who always looked like a walking disaster. Anyone who didn't know better would think that we were close friends.

"Taffy, I asked if you're going to Curtis's party," Mona said, interrupting my thoughts. "I hope so, because I am."

"I don't know yet," I answered. "I may have to audition for a television commercial Friday night." Then seeing the opportunity I had been looking for, I added, "Besides, Curtis will probably be the only boy there."

"Oh, no, he won't," Lisa said eagerly. "All the guys are going. Keith Masterson and Scott Daly and Randy Kirwan and . . ."

She was still naming off boys, but the instant she said Randy's name, I tuned her out. I didn't need to hear any more. If Randy would be at Curtis's party, then so would I! No matter how many auditions my mother might have set up. I would get a new outfit. Maybe a new hairstyle. All I had to do was convince my mother that I needed all that for a photo session or an audition or something. She would go along with anything if she thought it would help me get into show business. Still, I had to get busy and make plans. There were only three days left until the party—and my last chance to make the right impression on Randy before school started again in the fall. Handsome Randy. Wonderful Randy. The boy of my dreams.

I stood in the hot-lunch line at noon and watched Jana and her friends out of the corner of my eye. They always brought their lunches, so they went right to their table instead of standing in line. They always sat at the same table, too. One in the corner where they could watch everybody else and talk about them. Today they were talking about me. Me and my diary.

I could tell by the way they stopped giggling every so often and looked in my direction. Then they would put their heads together and start giggling again.

I couldn't believe how slowly the lunch line was moving. I tried to ignore them, even though my ears were burning, and concentrate on the choices at the steam tables ahead of me. Meat loaf. Yuk. Fish sticks. Gross. The only thing that looked good was the chocolate pudding.

I paid for the dish of chocolate pudding and a carton of milk and looked around for someplace to sit. Jana and her friends were still at their table. I certainly didn't want to sit with them. Sometimes I sat with Alexis Duvall and her friends, but today her table was full. Lisa and Sara and Kim and Marcie and even Mona were sitting there. I would have squeezed in at their table if only one of them had looked up and smiled at me or waved me over, but no one did. I sighed and pretended not to notice them either. They were just like all the other girls in Mark Twain Elementary, jealous of my looks and my new career in modeling and television.

I stood there holding my tray and feeling like an idiot for absolutely ages before I spotted an empty table by the door. It was beside the garbage can, and sometimes when kids threw away lunch bags or apple cores and their aim was bad, the stuff landed on that table. That's why it was empty. I didn't care. There was nothing on it today, and I could sit with my back to the rest of the cafeteria.

Jana and her friends can talk about me all they want to, I thought as I nibbled at my chocolate pudding. I'll show them a thing or two at Curtis Trowbridge's party Friday night. I'll be so gorgeous that Randy Kirwan won't be able to take his eyes off me. And I'll talk to him, somewhere in a dark corner where we can be alone, and I'll be so sweet and so nice that—

"Hey, Taffy."

The voice interrupted my dream just as I was getting to the best part. I glared at Beth Barry, who was standing beside my table, smiling and looking innocent. Her other friends were there, too, pitching their lunch garbage into the trash.

"What do you want?" I muttered.

"I just wondered if you got your dirty magazine back," she said, and then snickered. "Since it didn't have your name on it, we put it on the table with all the other leftovers, and when I looked for it at recess, it was gone."

"That was not mine, and you know it," I said.

I could feel my anger rising toward the danger point. How dare she say a thing such as that? Besides, Beth knew as well as I did that Miss Wiggins would never leave a magazine such as that on a table in her classroom.

"But you said that you lost something important," insisted Jana.

Jumping to my feet, I glared straight at her. "You know very well that it was my diary and not—" I stopped cold, slapping my hand over my mouth the instant I realized what I had said. I hadn't meant to say a thing such as that. How could I have slipped? How could I have let them trick me?

Melanie gasped. "Your DIARY!" she shrieked so loudly that kids all over the cafeteria were stopping what they were doing and looking at us.

"I was just kidding," I said quickly. Then I shrugged and tried to act casual, as if I couldn't care less about what they thought.

"Sure you were," said Katie, and she exchanged knowing looks with Christie. "Of course, you *really* lost it," she went on as if that were the only thing that made sense, "and you're scared to death that whoever has it will read it."

"Yeah," Beth added, grinning deliciously at me

over her shoulder as she and the others headed for the door. "And tell the whole world the *truth* about Taffy Sinclair."

I stood there watching them leave the cafeteria. The chocolate pudding was swirling around nauseously in my stomach. Little did they know, I thought, just how true those words were. I had written everything in my diary. I had told it all my secrets as if I were talking to my best friend. My thoughts. My feelings about everybody, including Randy Kirwan. Not only that, I had written all about my troubles with Jana Morgan and The Fabulous Five.

5 ✽

Word that my diary was missing spread like wildfire. On the playground after lunch kids were looking at me and some were even pointing and giggling. Jana and her friends were the worst. They didn't even wait to go out by the fence to gather into a huddle and start whispering. I knew what they were whispering about. Me and my lost diary. I also knew that they had it. Otherwise, why did they make such a big deal of mentioning that they had found a dirty magazine? I was sure that they had really found that magazine, too, and were using it to cover up the fact that they had my private, personal property.

BETSY HAYNES

I whirled around and hurried back inside the building, walking fast so that they would think I had important business. I hoped they would think I was going to the office to tell on them. But as soon as I got around the corner and out of sight of the front door, I crumpled against the wall and closed my eyes. I had to find a way to get my diary back before they read it and decided to get even with me for what I had written.

Suddenly I was flooded with memories.

Dear Diary:

Today was the most wonderful day of my life. Today I caught Jana Morgan doing something that could get her into a lot of trouble.

Miss Wiggins told our class that her wallet was missing. After school I walked into the girls' bathroom and there was Jana—hiding the wallet. I thought about telling on her. She would get into so much trouble, and it would serve her right! It would pay her back for all the mean things she has done to me.

But then I got a better idea. In fact it's the greatest idea I've ever had. I'm going to blackmail her!!!

I cringed when I remembered that entry in my diary and realized all the trouble I could get into. I *had* blackmailed Jana. Just the way I had said I would, but things had worked out very differently than I had expected.

> *Dear Diary:*
> *At first blackmailing Jana was a lot of fun. I made her do my math homework every day. She hated that, and all I could do was laugh.*
> *But then Alexis noticed us talking together a lot and asked me if Jana and I had started to be friends. She said she thought it was super since we had been enemies for so long.*
> *I hadn't really thought about people's thinking we were friends. But the more I thought about it, the more I liked the idea. I can't explain why. I just did. That's when I started blackmailing her even more. I made her carry my lunch tray and walk around the playground with me.*

Other kids noticed us together, too, including Randy Kirwan. He was horsing around on the playground when we walked by, but he stopped and watched us. I had been dying to know exactly what he was thinking.

I sighed. It wouldn't make any difference if anyone thought Jana and I were friends—not if Jana showed that part of my diary to Miss Wiggins or to Mrs. Winchell, the school principal. After all, Jana hadn't stolen the wallet. She had found it. And blackmailing is a crime. They might call the police, and I might get sent to jail or to reform school.

As I stood there, I heard the front door open and then footsteps heading up the hall in my direction. What if it was Jana? What if she had followed me into the school to tell me that she had my diary and that she had already opened it and read it—especially the part about being blackmailed? What if she was on her way to show it to Mrs. Winchell at this very instant?

Panic. I looked around. What could I say I was doing in the deserted school during lunch period? Where could I hide? There wasn't time to run down the hall and duck into the girls' bathroom. Besides, Jana would know I was running away from her if I did that.

I took a deep breath. I wouldn't give Jana Morgan the satisfaction of thinking that she was getting to me, even though she definitely was. Slowly I opened my shoulder bag and began rummaging around in it, trying to give the impression that I was doing something very important. I would have to distract her, get her mind off the diary, I thought as I listened to the steps coming closer.

I know! I decided with a smile. Jana is so jealous of me she can hardly stand it. She pretends she isn't, but she is. I'll just tell her that I have to call one of the local television stations—no, I'll say a national network—about my big audition and that I'm looking in my purse for the number. My smile turned into a delicious laugh. That should do it.

"Hi, Taffy. What's so funny?"

My heart almost stopped as Randy Kirwan came around the corner and stopped beside me. It wasn't Jana, after all. It was Randy, and he was giving me a gorgeous smile. Had *he* followed me into the building? Had he seen me come inside and decided that it was the perfect chance to talk to me? Alone?

I had to think fast. "Nothing's really funny," I said, smiling back at him. "I was just trying to imagine what Curtis's party will be like Friday night. I think it's going to be a ball. I can hardly wait."

Randy looked surprised. "You're going? That's terrific. But Curtis was telling everybody that you couldn't come because you had to try out for some television commercial or something like that."

"Oh, I'll be there," I assured him. "In fact, that's why I came into the school. I have to call the TV station and tell them I can't audition Friday night because I have something much more important to do. I'm looking for their phone number. It's somewhere in my purse."

I was trying as hard as I could to look casual, to act as if this sort of thing happened every day, but my hand was shaking so badly that I plunged it into my purse.

When I looked at Randy again, his eyes were glowing with admiration. "Wow. Do you mean that you would give up something as important as a chance to be on television again just to come to a party?"

"Of course." I could feel my confidence rising. Randy thought I was special. He didn't even have to say it out loud for me to know. I wondered for a fleeting moment if my hair looked okay. Then I flashed an even bigger smile and said, "This isn't just an ordinary party. All my *best* friends are going to be there."

I don't know if he got the message that I meant him when I said that my best friends would be there or not, because just then Scott Daly charged down the hall yelling to Randy that a game of touch tag was starting on the playground.

After the two of them left, I stood there tingling all over as I thought about what Randy and I had just said to each other. He was glad that I was going to the party! He even thought I was special for giving up an audition to go.

I had to go to Curtis's party. That's all there was to it. It could be the most important night of my life. There were only two things that could spoil it. Two *big* things. The television audition—if I couldn't convince my mother to let me go to the party instead. And my diary—if I couldn't get it back before Friday night.

6 ❄

"Taffy, I know it seems important to you now, dear, but believe me, when you're a famous star you won't even remember some silly old sixth-grade graduation party. It won't matter to you one bit that you missed it. In fact, you'll be grateful to me for insisting that you audition for that television commercial instead. Taffy, love, didn't you hear me? You're going to be a star!"

I stared down at my feet so that my mother wouldn't see the tears welling up in my eyes. When I got home from my ballet lesson, she had met me at the door with the news. Now we were sitting in the family room with all the autographed pictures of

40

famous stars the Rockettes had appeared with hanging on the walls. People such as Frank Sinatra and Barbra Streisand and Robert Redford, and she was saying that the television station wanted to audition me at eight o'clock Friday evening—right in the middle of Curtis's party.

"But, Mother," I insisted for the umpteenth time. "Can't we postpone it? Can't I audition Saturday morning instead? I promise I'll get up early and be there when the station opens. Oh, please?"

"In the morning? When your eyes are all puffy? And besides, I have it on good authority that Cynthia Cameron is going to audition, too, and you know she's your biggest competition. If you don't look your best, she'll get the job instead of you."

"My eyes are hardly ever puffy in the morning," I argued, ignoring the bit about Cynthia Cameron. I would deal with her later. "Besides, all my friends are going to be at that party."

A look of pain crossed her face, and she glanced up at the picture of Barbra Streisand on the wall above her. It said, "Best of everything to Sally Starre (that was my mother's stage name) from Barbra."

"After all I've tried to do for you," she said, sniffing back tears and looking at me again. "All the sacrifices

I've made so that my only daughter could have the show business career that I gave up when I got married. And this is the thanks I get. You can't even miss one, insignificant little party when it could mean the big break we've been waiting for."

Some big break, I thought. It was just a commercial for the local television station advertising their summer lineup of children's programs. From the way my mother was acting, you would have thought that it would be shown across the country on all the major networks. She should have been an actress instead of a dancer with the Radio City Music Hall Rockettes, I thought with a sigh. But she wasn't an actress. She was my mother, and I could see that our conversation was going nowhere. There was only one thing to do. Go along with her until I could think of a new approach.

Later, in my room, I tried to do my homework, but all I could think about was Randy Kirwan and the way he had followed me into the school at noon. I was certain that he had been waiting for the right moment to talk to me about Curtis's party. A moment when we could be alone. And now my mother was going to ruin everything by insisting that I go to the television audition instead of the party. She was at least going to *try* to ruin everything. No, I thought, shaking my head sadly. She wasn't actually trying to ruin things for me. She thought that what she was doing was for the best. It's just that sometimes what seemed the best to her was really the worst for me.

I drummed my fingers on my desk excitedly. This was only Tuesday. Anything could happen between now and the party Friday night. And something would. I would see to that. A plan was already forming in my mind.

I raced through my homework. I had something important to do, and the sooner I got started, the better. Throwing open my closet door, I jerked things off the hangers as fast as I could and pitched them onto my bed. Tops. Skirts. Jeans. Then I sauntered casually into the living room where my parents were watching television. I was about to put part one of my plan to work.

"Mother. Would you come here a moment? I need some advice."

Since I hardly ever ask her for advice, she sprang up from the sofa. "What is it, dear?" she asked eagerly.

I led her into my bedroom, then put my hands on my hips and sighed loudly as I nodded toward the mess on my bed. "I've tried on absolutely everything I own, and *nothing* will do for my big audition Friday night. I just don't know what I'm going to wear."

Mother looked surprised for an instant and then began picking through the things strewn across my bed. "Here," she said, holding up my favorite blue outfit, the one with the knee-length pants and ruffled top that matched my eyes exactly. "You look gorgeous in this. I remember when you wore it to the Fourth of July parade last summer. You were stunning!"

"That's just it," I insisted. "That's *last* year's outfit. You know as well as I do that Cynthia Cameron will have on something new. She's bound to show up in an outfit that's the very latest."

I could tell instantly that I had gotten through to her. Cynthia Cameron was my age and lived in Monroe, a town a few miles north of Bridgeport, and she had tried out for the same part in *Interns and Lovers* that I had played on television. Of course I got the part, but ever since then her mother and mine had been enemies as terrible as Jana Morgan and me. If there was anything that would convince my mother to buy me a new outfit, it was the mention of Cynthia Cameron's name.

"Maybe you're right," Mother mused. "It might be a good idea to go out to the mall after school tomorrow and see what we can find." She paused a moment and then beamed at me. "After all, we both know how important Friday night is, don't we?"

"That's right, Mother." I crossed my fingers and held them behind my back. "Friday night could be one of the most important nights of my life."

7 ✣

*N*ow that part one of my plan had gone just as I had hoped, the next thing I had to do was get my diary back. This called for part two of my plan.

I left for school fifteen minutes early the next morning so that I could head off Mona Vaughn a block from the playground. I would rather have called her the night before and talked to her in total privacy, but meeting her would have to do. Her parents didn't have much money, and a telephone was a luxury they couldn't afford. Luxury? I wondered. How could anyone consider something so important as a telephone a luxury? But those had been Mona's very words when she had explained the situation to me a few weeks before.

Standing there waiting for her, I had time to think about my diary again. I would die, absolutely *die*, if Jana and the others read it. Or worse yet, if they took it to the party and read it out loud in front of everybody. I knew exactly what they would do. They would pick out the parts that would embarrass me the most. Parts such as what I said about the club they had against me.

Dear Diary:

Today I found out something awful. It has been bad enough that Jana and her friends hate me and are jealous of my looks, but today I found out that they have a club against me. It's called The Against Taffy Sinclair Club, and the purpose of the club is to spy on me and write down everything I do and then get together and talk about me. I think that's the meanest thing I ever heard of!!!

It would be embarrassing for everyone to know about that club, all right, but that wasn't the worst of it. The rest of what I wrote was even more humiliating.

Dear Diary:
Today I did something to get even with Jana for having a club against me. I told her that I have a club against her, too. I said that it is called The Against Jana Morgan Club. What I didn't tell her was that I am the only member.

I shifted my books nervously. Now Jana would know the truth. She had always thought that I had other girls in my club. She thought that at least Mona Vaughn was in it because Mona always followed me around like a lost puppy. I wished now that Mona *had* been in my club. I wished that I had asked every other girl in our class to be in it. I had wished it then, too.

Dear Diary:
Today I saw Jana and her friends writing things about me in their notebooks. It made me furious. I really wish I had other girls in my club, too, so that we could talk about them and write things in our notebooks. We could write about how Jana always

makes goo-goo eyes at Mr. Neal, the fifth-grade teacher, or how flat-chested she and her friends are compared to me. I could write those things myself, but it wouldn't be any fun. Not without someone to share them with. I thought about asking some girls to be in my club. I've thought about it a lot lately, but I couldn't stand for anyone *to think that I had to beg someone to be my friend.*

Actually, most girls were too jealous of me to want to be friends, I thought. Everyone, that is, except for Mona Vaughn. Fortunately The Fabulous Five liked Mona, too. That's why right now she was my only hope.

When Mona walked up the street, I was so deep in thought that I didn't even see her coming.

"Hi, Taffy," she said cheerfully. "Waiting for someone?"

"Oh, hi." I looked around to make sure no one from school was nearby to hear what we were saying. "As a matter of fact, I was waiting for you."

Mona was obviously pleased. She danced up to me, grinning like crazy. I looked her over quickly. Actually, her dark hair did look better now that Jana and her friends had shown her how to style it. And her violet eyes were finally visible with her bangs pulled away from her face. But she still looked like the pits with her baggy, mismatched clothes and her dingy sneakers. I had been counting on that to make my plan work.

"I really like the way you're wearing your hair lately," I said. "That's a neat style."

Mona looked a little embarrassed for a moment. "Thanks," she murmured. "Jana and her friends showed me how to fix it this way."

"They've really been buttering you up lately, haven't they?" I asked, trying to sound innocent.

"Buttering me up? Of course not. What makes you think that?"

"Oh, nothing." I didn't say anything else for a minute, and then I added as casually as I could, "They were really hanging around with you a lot for a while, weren't they? You know, when Melanie Edwards and I were in the same modeling class and were spending so much time together. I'm sure they weren't trying to make me jealous, or anything. They probably just like you."

Mona's eyes widened in horror, but she kept looking straight ahead and didn't say anything. She probably didn't think I saw the expression on her

THE TRUTH ABOUT TAFFY SINCLAIR 51

face. She probably didn't think that Jana and the others would do something so mean to anyone, either. But of course I knew better. Just look at all the mean things they had done to me.

When I saw Mona's chin start to quiver, I knew it was time to bring up my diary.

"They just love to act goody-goody and then do terrible things behind people's backs," I said. Mona shot a questioning look in my direction, so I went on. "For instance, did you know that they are the ones who have my diary, and they won't give it back?"

"You're kidding! I heard on the playground that it was missing. But how do you know that they're the ones who have it?"

"I saw them with it," I said triumphantly. "They were crowded around looking at it yesterday morning when we found the lockers all mixed up. It was just before Miss Wiggins told everybody to give back what they could identify."

"Maybe they didn't know it was yours."

"They knew, all right," I said. "Not only that, I asked them for it, but they wouldn't give it to me. Now they've probably hidden it somewhere, but I don't have the slightest idea where."

"Oh, Taffy. That's terrible. Maybe I could find out for you."

I sighed deeply and gave her a hug. "Thanks a lot, Mona, but it's no use. Even though they *really* like you and trust you, I'm sure they wouldn't tell even you where they're keeping it. They want to make me as miserable as they possibly can!"

Mona started to protest, but I shook my head. "Forget it," I said with a sad little smile. "I know that there isn't anything you can do. But thanks anyway. I appreciate your wanting to help. Let's change the subject and talk about something fun, like Curtis's party. Do you know yet what you're wearing?"

This time her expression turned dismal, and she gazed dejectedly toward her feet. "I don't have anything to wear," she admitted. "Not anything nice enough for a party. I was even thinking about not going."

"Don't be silly. Of course you're going. You don't need anything special for Curtis's party. Probably most girls will be in jeans."

"So?" said Mona. "These are my best jeans, and they're patched in three places."

"So?" I teased. "Patched jeans are in. But wait. I have a better idea. I have tons of clothes, and I can't wear them all to one party. Why don't you come over after supper and try on some things? I'll bet we could find the perfect outfit for you. Okay?"

"Do you mean it?" she asked, but before I could answer, she added, "But I couldn't. I mean, your clothes are so . . . so *beautiful*."

"They're just clothes," I reassured her. "Besides, you and I are friends."

Mona's eyes were shining with such gratitude that I knew instantly that she would do everything in her power to get my diary back for me.

8 ❊

I left Mona at the entrance to the school ground, saying that I had to look over my spelling words one more time before the bell rang. Actually, I wanted to make sure she had the chance to talk to Jana and her friends about my diary before she changed her mind or chickened out. Besides, the sooner I got it back, the better.

Just as I had predicted, she went straight over to the girls who were standing in their special spot by the fence. I leaned against a tree and opened my notebook to my spelling words, holding it up so that I could look over the top and watch without anyone's realizing what I was doing.

54

Melanie was the first one to notice Mona walking toward them, and as soon as Melanie waved and called to her, the others acted glad to see her, too. I breathed a sigh of relief as they gathered around her and started talking. If anyone could find out about my diary, Mona could.

It was all I could do to lower my eyes and pretend to be looking at my spelling words. I had to stay cool and keep *anyone* from suspecting that I was spying on The Fabulous Five.

I counted to ten and looked over the top of the notebook again. They were still talking. They were even laughing. What was that all about? There wasn't anything funny about their *stealing* my diary. Having something that belonged to someone else and refusing to give it back was just the same as stealing, I assured myself.

Maybe they were laughing about something that was written in my diary. I bit my lower lip and tried to think what it could be. I remembered some more problems I'd had with Jana and what I had written about them.

Dear Diary:
  Today Jana Morgan's friends are mad at her, and

I'm pretending to be her friend. I couldn't believe that she actually fell for it and even said yes when I offered to teach her how to use body language to send messages to cute boys. Boy, was that funny!!! Her body language looked like baby talk.

I started giggling when I thought about how I had tricked her. She really had looked pretty strange when she wiggled her hips and batted her eyes at every cute boy in sixth grade. And Miss Wiggins had even seen her doing it and asked her if she felt okay. Yipes! I thought. Jana wouldn't laugh if she read that. And she certainly wouldn't tell anyone else about it. She'd be steaming mad.

I gulped and checked out The Fabulous Five and Mona again. They weren't laughing now, either. They were huddled close together talking, but I couldn't see their faces clearly enough to tell if they were happy or mad.

Looking away again, I began to worry about something else. If Jana really had read my diary, then she would know about all the things I had written about Mona. A shiver crept along my spine. I had only written the truth. And I never meant for *anyone* to see it, especially not Mona.

Dear Diary:

You should have seen how Mona Vaughn looked today. Her clothes were so old and ugly that she looked like a bag lady.

Well, she did! I thought, as tears spurted into my eyes. It was the truth, but that didn't mean she could help it. It didn't mean she wanted to look that way, either. It just meant that was how she looked!

I cringed as I remembered another entry I had made a few days later.

Dear Diary:

I don't know how Mona Vaughn can stand to be seen in public. Today she had on slacks that must have been three sizes too big and a sweatshirt with a hole in one elbow.

I'll bet she buys her clothes at the Salvation Army store. What is even worse, she doesn't seem to realize how embarrassing it is for me when people see us together.

This time my knees got weak. How would I ever explain a thing such as that to Mona? Jana would be just mean enough to show it to her, too, I thought.

Jumping to attention, I looked back at the spot by the fence where they had been standing a moment before, but now they were gone. I scanned the playground, but I couldn't see them anywhere. How could they have disappeared so quickly? Where did they go?

I had to find out what was going on, so I closed my notebook and raced toward the building as fast as I could. Maybe Jana had taken Mona to show her where she kept the diary hidden. Maybe it was in her locker or in her desk in the sixth-grade room. Wherever it was, I had to follow them and find out for myself. Somehow I'd have to find a way to keep Mona from reading it and taking sides with The Fabulous Five.

Hurrying up the front steps, I had just reached out to open the front door when someone lunged in front of me.

"Hi, Taffy!"

It was Clarence Marshall, and he had a ridiculous grin on his face and a shock of dingy blond hair hanging in his eyes. As usual, one side of his shirt was tucked into his pants, but the other side was hanging out.

"Hey, I just heard that you're going to Curtis Trowbridge's party, after all. I think that's great. I'm going, too."

"Gross," I muttered under my breath, even though I didn't really care if Clarence heard it or not. He was the most obnoxious boy in Mark Twain Elementary, and I wouldn't be the least bit sorry if he got held back and couldn't go on to junior high with the rest of us next year.

"Would you move?" I asked impatiently. "I need to get inside. It's important."

"I even heard that Curtis's parents won't be home," he said, completely ignoring the fact that I had asked him to move.

"Will you get out of my way!" I demanded. "I said I need to get inside the school."

"It'll cost you a kiss at Curtis's party," he said slyly.

The instant he said that I shuddered, remembering how he had chased me around Kim Baxter's swimming pool last summer until he caught me and plastered a sloppy kiss on the side of my face. I'd die if he ever did that again.

"Clarence Marshall, I wouldn't kiss you if you were the last boy on earth. Now, get out of my way before I call Mrs. Winchell."

Clarence moved, but he was still looking at me with an insolent grin on his face. I pushed past him and hurried into the building and down the hall toward the sixth-grade lockers just as the first bell rang.

I sighed. I was too late anyway, thanks to Clarence. If Mona and The Fabulous Five had been there, they were already gone.

I let myself be pushed along by the avalanche of kids that came roaring through the halls as soon as the bell sounded. I hardly even noticed the pushing and shoving and the yelling and screaming as I thought about my diary and the consequences I might face if anyone read it.

No one would understand. They would think that I was a mean and spiteful person who picked on practically everybody. That wasn't true. In fact, it was the opposite of the truth. Everybody picked on me. Or they would, if I would let them.

I hurried down the hall, fighting back tears. My mother had said that kids were jealous of me and that I should hold my head up high and act as if it didn't matter, and that's what I always tried to do. Like ignoring it when someone stared at me. Or pretend-ing I didn't hear it when kids whispered behind my back. But even though I did those things just the way she told me, nothing ever seemed to help. Nothing! The truth was, nobody liked me. Nobody except Mona Vaughn, and now because I had written the truth about how she dressed in my private, personal diary, I had probably blown that, too.

9 ❋

If Mona had gotten the chance to read my diary, she didn't give herself away in class. She even smiled at me when she came into the room. I looked again at her patched jeans and faded blouse and felt a rush of guilt over what I had written about her. She had less than any other girl in sixth grade. Why wasn't she jealous of me like everyone else?

Miss Wiggins jumped up from her desk the second the bell rang. She was smiling so brightly that I wondered for an instant if she was as happy that school was about to be out as we were.

"Class," she chirped. "This morning we are going

to dispense with our regular lessons and do a little housecleaning in preparation for the end of the school year."

A cheer went up all over the room. We would do practically anything to get out of lessons, even housecleaning.

Then she pushed two shoe boxes into the center of her desk, pulled off their lids with a ceremonious flourish and announced, "I am going to divide up the chores in a democratic way. In the box on my left"— she paused and pointed to that box—"are all the jobs we need to get done. And in the box on my right"— again she paused, pointing to the appropriate box— "are all of your names. When I pull out a job, I'll also pull out the names of the team who will do it. Now, isn't that fair?"

Nobody said anything, and a few kids groaned. I wanted to groan, too, but I didn't. It would be just my luck to get stuck with someone like Curtis Trowbridge or Clarence Marshall. I also noticed The Fabulous Five exchanging worried looks. They were so snobby that they would probably die if they didn't get on teams together.

"The first job," Miss Wiggins went on, "is to straighten the art cabinet."

That would be easy, I thought, cleaning brushes and throwing away dried-out jars of poster paint. I crossed my fingers that she would call my name, but of course she didn't.

"Sara Sawyer and Melanie Edwards," she announced.

Miss Wiggins dug back into the boxfull of jobs and pulled out another one. "The second job is to return material to the Media Center."

I drummed my fingertips on my desk in boredom while she reached into the other box for names. That was an easy one, too, so of course I wouldn't get it.

"Randy Kirwan and Taffy Sinclair."

I jumped straight up in my seat when I heard my name, and my heart jumped even higher. Randy and I? Together? It was too wonderful to be true.

When I glanced back at Randy to give him a big smile, my gaze was stopped cold by five pairs of eyes. Every member of The Fabulous Five was glaring at me, and if looks could kill, I'd be dead. I didn't care. I gave them my big smile instead and turned around to listen to Miss Wiggins assign the rest of the jobs.

"Now, you two, this is what I want you to do," she said a few minutes later. Randy and I were side by side at her desk, and I was trying my best to listen, but I couldn't help wondering how we looked standing there together. "There are three stacks of books on the top shelf in the reading corner and several stacks of maps and papers on the table that need to go back to Mrs. Birney in the Media Center. She will know what to do with them. All you have to do is take them to her."

"Okay, Miss Wiggins, that will be easy," said Randy. Then he grinned at me and added, "I'll carry the books since they're heavier."

Kids were scurrying all over the room starting their jobs as we loaded up to make our first trip to the Media Center. Jana stuck her nose into the air and went to work washing the front chalkboard. I knew that she was just pretending not to see us.

As soon as we stepped into the hall my heart started to pound. I was totally alone with Randy Kirwan. Our footsteps echoed as we walked along the deserted corridor, and I tried desperately to think of something to say.

My mind was blank. I couldn't believe such a thing could happen to me. I had never had trouble talking to boys in my life. In fact, boys were the easiest human beings in the world to talk to. It was *girls* who had always been the problem. But now when it was really important, my brain had turned to Silly Putty.

I sneaked a quick glance at Randy. He was walking along with that stack of books as if he didn't have a care in the world. I racked my brain, trying to remember all the dumb rules I had ever heard for making conversation with a boy.

Number one, ask about a school assignment. I couldn't do that. School would be out in a couple of days, and Wiggins had stopped giving assignments.

Number two, be funny. Tell jokes. Make him laugh. HA! At a time like this? Whoever made up that rule had to be kidding.

Rule three, compliment him. I swallowed hard. I could tell him how handsome he is. I could . . .

"Curtis says he has big plans for his party Friday night," said Randy, bringing me crashing back to reality.

"Really?" I said out loud, but my mind was screaming, *The party! Why didn't I think of that?* It only took me an instant to recover. "Well, I just hope that some of the rowdy kids don't get into trouble," I said slyly.

"Why do you say that?" asked Randy.

"Clarence Marshall says that Curtis's parents aren't going to be home." I laughed nervously.

Randy turned his big blue eyes on me for a moment, and my heart almost stopped. Was he going to say something about our being together at the party? Or even being alone together now that he knew Curtis's parents wouldn't be snooping around?

Shaking his head, he said, "Don't pay any attention to Clarence. You know how he is. He's always making up things to get attention. Alexis even said he's been going around telling all the girls that he wants to kiss them at Curtis's party. He's probably even said it to you."

I nodded and fought down a blush. This conversation wasn't going the way I wanted it to. I would have to think of another approach to get Randy to say something about our being together Friday night.

We had reached the Media Center, and Randy balanced his stack of books on one arm and opened the door for me. He was so polite. Not like some guys who were icky polite. Curtis Trowbridge, to mention one person in particular. Randy just did nice things for people as if they came natural to him.

After we left the things with Mrs. Birney and headed back to the sixth-grade room, my mind was whirring as I went over the rules for making conversation with a boy again. I might never get a more perfect opportunity, and there were only enough books and papers left for one more trip to the Media Center. The only trouble was, even if I thought of the perfect thing to say, it probably wouldn't do any good. Randy liked Jana. Everybody knew that, and whenever I closed my eyes and saw his face, hers was always there, too, making me miserable. Sometimes, when I was feeling especially miserable, I would write about it in my diary.

Dear Diary:

Today Randy took Jana to Mama Mia's for pizza after the football game. He didn't just sit with her when he got there. He asked her ahead of time, so it was a real date. And to make matters worse, everybody was there and saw them together.

Dear Diary:

It's Saturday night, and I'm really depressed. I

thought this time I had broken up Randy and Jana for sure. I thought I had fixed things so that he would ask me for a date to go to the movies with the rest of the gang. I was wrong. He asked her instead. They are together at this very minute and I'm home alone.

Dear Diary:

Randy Kirwan is the most wonderful boy in the world, but I don't understand why he likes Jana instead of me. I talk to him all the time to let him know how much I like him. I smile at him. What else can I do to make him see that it's me, *not Jana, who is the perfect girl for him?*

Just as we reached the classroom door, I got a brilliant idea. Randy liked to do nice things for people. It just came natural. Of course. That was it. I would ask him to do me a favor. And I had the perfect favor to ask him. I would have to stretch the truth a little, but it would be worth it. And if I worked it just right, he'd never be able to say no.

We loaded up with books and papers and started down the hall again. I took a deep breath to get up my nerve.

"You were right about Clarence wanting to kiss me," I began shyly. "In fact . . ." I let my voice trail off as if I couldn't stand to say any more.

Randy frowned. "What do you mean?"

"I haven't told anyone," I whispered. "Clarence is such a bully. But he's always following me after school. And trying to kiss me when no one's around."

"That creep." Randy stopped dead in his tracks. "Wait until I get my hands on him!"

"Oh, no. Don't tell him that I told you. He'll be really mad at me."

Randy stood there for a moment, and I could tell that he was thinking over what I had said. I could hardly breathe as I waited to see if my plan had worked.

"Okay," he said. "I won't tell him, but meet me by the front door after school. I'll walk you home, and I'll do it every day until school is out. Let's see Clarence try anything when I'm with you."

My feet didn't touch the floor all the way to the Media Center and back. It had worked! Randy was going to walk me home from school for the rest of the week. Surely by the party Friday night he'd be my boyfriend instead of Jana Morgan's. I would take him away from her if it was the last thing I ever did, and there wasn't a thing she could do about it.

10 ✻

"Jana and the others say they don't have your diary," said Mona when I met her in the girls' bathroom during morning recess.

"Ha!" I scoffed. "What did I tell you? They won't admit it to you because they know you and I are friends."

"Are you really sure they have it? What if they're telling the truth? I'll bet someone else has it and is planning to give it back."

"Of course I'm sure they have it," I insisted. "Who else would keep it hidden all this time? Anyone else would have given it back a long time ago."

Mona shrugged and looked dejected.

"That's okay, Mona. You tried." I made my voice sound as sad as possible. "I'll just have to think of *something* before it's too late."

"What do you mean, 'before it's too late'?"

"Oh, I was just thinking that they are probably planning something. Something awful . . . like reading my diary out loud at Curtis's party Friday night."

I could see from the look on Mona's face that she was surprised. "They wouldn't do a thing like that. Would they?"

"Not to you," I said. "Or to anybody else except me. You know how much they hate me. They always have. And now that I'm probably going to get that part in the television commercial, they hate me more than ever."

Mona was quiet for a moment. "Let me talk to them again. If they have your diary, I'll find out this time. I promise."

After Mona left, I put my elbows on the shelf above the sinks and stared at myself in the mirror. Was it possible that Jana and her friends really didn't have my diary? It would have been a lucky break for them if it had landed in one of their lockers during the mix-up. But there were twenty-one other kids in Miss

Wiggins's sixth-grade class, twenty if I didn't count myself, who could have gotten that diary just as easily as one of The Fabulous Five.

In my mind I went down each row in the classroom looking for possibilities. Kids who would have a reason to keep my diary. Matt Zeboski—no. Gloria Drexler—no. Sara Sawyer—probably not. We weren't great friends, but we weren't big enemies, either. Keith Masterson—no. Wait a minute, I thought. Keith and Joel and Richie were the ones who messed up the lockers. Maybe one of them had it. They were always playing jokes on people. I made a mental note that the three of them were suspects, and then went on down the rows. Of course every one of The Fabulous Five had to be counted. Alexis and Kim and Lisa were maybe's along with Sara.

Suddenly I thought about Mona. She was the one who had actually taken the money from Miss Wiggins's wallet. Besides that, she had more to gain than anybody from reading my diary. Wasn't she always following me around and trying to be friends? Wasn't she the homeliest girl in the sixth grade? It made sense that she might want my diary to try to find out my secrets. Not my personal secrets, like everyone else, but my *beauty secrets*!

I smiled at my reflection in the mirror. Maybe that's why she was so sure that I was going to get it back. I remembered her words: *I'll bet someone else has it and is planning to give it back*. She's only going to keep it for a little while. Just long enough to read it. Oh, my gosh, I thought. If she has it, she won't find what she expects to find in it.

I stood there for another couple of minutes, thinking over the situation. In some ways Mona was the obvious one, since she had stolen something before. But on the other hand, if Mona had it, she would have opened it by now, and she certainly wouldn't be acting so friendly to me if she had read it. Jana and her friends had to be the ones. They have my diary, I thought. That's all there is to it.

Even though recess was almost over, I sauntered out onto the playground. The weather had turned warm and most kids were just sitting around in groups talking instead of running and playing. Even the sixth-grade boys were standing quietly beside the ball diamond. I looked at Randy. He was so handsome standing there talking to his friends. I wondered if he would tell any of them that he was walking me home after school to protect me from Clarence Marshall. Probably not. He never bragged about himself, but the thought made me tingle with anticipation, anyway. It was hours and hours until school was out for the day. How could I stand it until then?

So what if I had stretched the truth about Clarence a little bit? No one would ever know the difference and . . .

"Hey, Taffy. Are you going to kiss me at Curtis's party Friday night?"

My mouth dropped open as Clarence came skidding up and stopped in front of me. I couldn't help wondering for an instant if he had some sort of ESP and knew that I was thinking about him and that was why he had rushed up to me just now.

"Don't be *weird*!" I said in an icy voice. "I've already told you. I wouldn't kiss you if you were the last boy on earth. Now leave me alone."

Clarence laughed and then went bounding off in the direction of a group of girls. He's probably going to bug them about kissing him, too, I thought angrily as I turned my back on him. He was such a jerk.

I was still grumbling to myself about Clarence when I got back to the room after recess, and I was almost to my seat when I noticed that someone had left a note on my desk. Terrific, I thought excitedly.

Maybe it's from Mona and she has some news about my diary.

I grabbed the note and practically tore the paper in my excitement to get it open. Then, spreading it out on my desk, I swallowed hard. It wasn't good news from Mona. It wasn't good news from anybody. It was a picture. The skin on the back of my neck began to crawl as I stared at the crude drawing of a book with a strap connecting the front to the back. And stared at the word "Diary" written across the cover. Beneath the drawing was a message scrawled in large capital letters.

FRIDAY NIGHT

Oh, no! I gasped. My worst fears were coming true.

11 *

I crumpled the paper in my hand and stuffed it into a pocket, and I tried to figure out what to do. Jana was out to get me, all right. If I ever had any doubts, they were gone now. *Friday Night*, the note said. Zero hour. Doomsday. The end of Taffy Sinclair.

There had to be something I could do to stop her. But what? It had been a mistake to rely on Mona. She had tried, but there wasn't anything she could do. Besides, Jana hated me too much to miss a golden opportunity such as this.

I had to find the diary, and suddenly as I sat there thinking the situation over, I knew the first place to look. My hand shot into the air.

"Yes, Taffy," said Miss Wiggins.

"May I leave the room, please?"

Miss Wiggins frowned. "But you just came in from recess."

"I know, but . . ." I stammered. I could feel my face turning pink. Why hadn't I waited a few more minutes?

"Well, if you're certain it's an emergency," Miss Wiggins warned.

"Oh, yes, Miss Wiggins. It's an emergency."

As I slid out of my seat I heard Joel Murphy whisper in a singsong voice, "We know where you're going." A bunch of other kids giggled.

I headed for the sixth-grade lockers the instant I got into the hall. Why had it taken me so long to figure it out? Jana wouldn't dare carry my diary into the classroom even if she hid it among her other books. It was a bright shade of blue, and it would be impossible to hide. No, I thought happily, it was probably in her locker where she and her friends could sneak it out to the fence during recess or at noon and read it and have a good laugh. Well, I thought, I'll put a stop to that. I could get inside her locker easily now that all the locks had been turned in to Miss

Wiggins, and I would fix her for stealing my property. I would steal it back.

The hinges on her locker door squealed loudly as I pulled it open in the silent corridor. I froze and darted quick glances out of the corner of each eye to see if anyone had heard. They hadn't. I waited a few more seconds just to be sure and then eased the door the rest of the way open without making any more noise. After one more check of the hall in each direction, I looked inside Jana's locker. Schoolbooks. A mirror hanging on the vent. A few papers. That was it. No diary. Not even anything blue.

My heart sank. What if she was keeping it at home? I would never be able to get it back then. Or else, I thought slyly, or else what if one of her friends has it for safekeeping? Then it could still be in one of the lockers, and I could still get it back.

I closed Jana's locker door very carefully and tiptoed up the hall to Beth's locker. Beth was Jana's best friend and the logical one to keep it for her. I would have bet almost anything that I was about to find it there. But the diary wasn't in Beth's locker, either. Or in Melanie's. Or Katie's. Or Christie's.

It isn't anywhere! I thought desperately. What am I going to do?

I leaned against the bank of lockers and rested my head against the cool metal. I tried not to think about what was going to happen Friday night, but I couldn't help it. I knew what everyone would think of me when they heard the things I had written in that diary. I knew they wouldn't understand.

In fact, nobody had ever understood me. They had always listened to Jana because she was so popular. Still, I had to admit, there were some things I didn't want people to understand. Some of my feelings were just too personal and too private. That's why I had written about them in my diary. Writing them down usually made me feel better. It helped me sort things out, and it was a little like talking things over with a friend, the kind of friend who never laughed and always understood. For instance, there was the time when I was appearing in *Interns and Lovers* on television and Jana wrote that awful article about me for the *Mark Twain Sentinel*. In it she said terrible things about me and called me the "queen of the soaps." I was so humiliated that I stayed home from school for days . . . writing in my diary.

Dear Dairy:
  Today was the most embarrassing day of my life.

Right there, on the front page of the school paper, was an article about me. Jana Morgan wrote it, and it was full of lies. I'll never go back to school. Nobody can make me face those kids again.

Dear Diary:

I didn't go to school again today. How can I when everyone acts so mean? My mother says it's because they're jealous of my looks. Well, I've got news for them. They think I like being pretty, but I don't. Not all the time, anyway.

And what's more, they probably think that I really want to be a model or a television star. Boy, would they be shocked if they knew that I don't want that, either. I'd give anything if I could stop being different and just be like everybody else.

Dear Diary:

I'm home again today. It's lonely, but it's better than being at school. I can't quit thinking about Jana Morgan. I can't stop wondering why she is jealous of me. She has everything! *She is popular and has tons of friends. And even more than that, she has Randy Kirwan, the boy of my dreams.*

And then there was the time I took the modeling class at Tanninger's Department Store. Jana and her friends took it, too. Melanie was so excited about becoming a model that she actually wanted to be friends with me to find out all my secrets. She knew I was the only other person in the class who stood a chance of getting a modeling job.

Anyway, at first I was friendly with Melanie because I knew it would drive the rest of The Fabulous Five wild to see us together and might even split up their gossipy club. But the more time I spent with Melanie, the more I liked being with her. I wrote about that in my diary, too.

Dear Diary:

I know it sounds crazy, but I'm beginning to think Melanie is a super person and a neat friend. We've started walking to school together and talking about modeling and clothes. It's great to have someone to talk with about those things.

Dear Diary:

I'm getting worried. Jana and her friends are trying to get Melanie back. I'll die if she goes back to being friends with them. I have to do something fast. Something that will convince Melanie that she needs me for a friend. But what?

I sighed. I had thought of something, all right, but it had backfired in my face the same way things had always backfired whenever I had tried to make friends. What's the use, anyway, I thought.

Suddenly I realized that I had been gone from the classroom for an awfully long time. Any minute now Miss Wiggins might come looking for me. As I hurried back up the hall I thought about Jana Morgan and my diary again. One thing was certain, I had to get it back. I couldn't let her read it out loud to the whole sixth grade. I had written too many things in it that *nobody* could ever know.

12 ✳

No matter how grim things seemed as far as my diary was concerned, I still had one thing to look forward to. Randy Kirwan was going to walk me home after school. The day seemed endless, even though we spent most of the time cleaning up the sixth-grade room to get it ready for summer vacation.

When the dismissal bell finally rang, I hurried to my locker and then to the front door to wait for Randy. I tried to look cool, even though my heart was racing. Maybe I should have stopped by the girls' bathroom and brushed my hair, I thought.

Mark Peters and Scott Daly walked by. They were Randy's best friends. I was hoping they would ask me whom I was waiting for, but they didn't.

Then Alexis Duvall and Lisa Snow came along next. "You just can't bear to walk out of good old Mark Twain Elementary after six long years, can you, Taffy?" Alexis said with a grin.

"Yeah," said Lisa. "It really gets to you, doesn't it?"

I nodded and smiled, wishing they would stop long enough to ask me what I was really doing waiting by the door, but of course they didn't. I glanced down the hall. If only Randy would hurry up. I was dying for someone to see us leaving the school together— especially Jana Morgan.

Instead, Clarence was lumbering toward the door. When he saw me, he started making smooching sounds and grinning broadly. "Just wait until Friday night!" he called as he went past.

Friday night. It depressed me even to think about it. Suddenly it didn't matter that Randy was walking me home. After Friday night he would probably think I was horrible and never want to speak to me again.

The school had almost emptied out by the time he finally got there. I tried to smile when I saw him coming, but I just didn't feel like it. Instead, I sighed and mumbled, "Hi," barely above a whisper.

"What's the matter? Has Clarence been bothering you again?"

I shook my head. It would be the truth if I told him what Clarence had said and that he had been making smooching noises. But even if Randy believed me now, he probably wouldn't after Jana read my diary out loud.

"Then what's the matter?" Randy repeated.

I thought quickly. "I guess I'm just a little sad about leaving our old school," I lied. "We've gone here all of our lives."

Randy nodded. "I'll miss it, too." Then he flashed a grin and added, "But don't tell anybody I said that. I don't want to get teased."

I said I wouldn't, and we walked along in silence. I knew I should be making fabulous conversation. I should be impressing Randy so that he would forget all about Jana Morgan and decide that he liked me instead. But for some reason I just couldn't. I didn't feel like talking. Not to Randy. Not to anybody.

When we got to my house, I thanked Randy for walking home with me and went inside. My mother was waiting for me.

"Hi, sweetheart. Are you ready to go to the mall and look for a new outfit for your audition Friday night?"

Surprise must have shown on my face because she added, "You didn't forget an important thing like that, did you? Just remember, Cynthia Cameron will do everything she can to get that job away from you."

"Sure, Mother. Let's go."

I followed her out to the car, thinking that usually shopping for new clothes at the mall was one of my favorite things to do. But today was different. And as we went from store to store, I couldn't seem to find anything I liked.

"What's wrong, love?" she asked after I left the fifth store without trying on a single thing. "You aren't coming down with something, are you?"

She stopped, turned me toward her, and studied my face. "You look a little pale. Here, let me feel your forehead for fever. It would be just *awful* if you got sick and missed the audition."

Dutifully, I let her feel my forehead. I knew I didn't have a fever, but it would make her feel better. Sometimes it seemed as if she cared more about my show business career than she did about me.

Finally we found an outfit that she felt sure would be just right. "It's perfect," she said as she handed it to the clerk at the cash register. "Cynthia Cameron can't possibly show up in anything that gorgeous. Oh, Taffy. Isn't it exciting? The job is yours. I can just feel it."

I tried to smile as I watched the clerk put the clothes into a bag. Mother was right about one thing. The outfit was pretty. It was a sundress with tiny straps and a full skirt that was a blaze of bright colors.

She was right about another thing, too, I thought. I would look great Friday night—when I met my doom.

Mona came over after supper. She was so shy about trying on my clothes that I had to talk her into it.

"But Taffy, they're all so beautiful," she said over and over.

"Here," I said, handing her my favorite blue knee pants and ruffled top. It was the same outfit my mother had suggested I wear to the audition before she agreed to buy me something new. "Try on this one. I think you'll look great in it."

Mona's eyes got big when she saw herself in the mirror. She really did look nice. Blue was a super color for her, and the pants and top couldn't have fit her any better.

"Wow!" she said. "Do you really mean that I can borrow this?"

"Of course. Not only that, because you look so nice in it, I think you ought to keep it."

Mona thanked me a million times before she left. She thanked me so much that it got embarrassing. "I'm really sorry I couldn't help you find your diary," she said as she headed out the door.

"That's okay," I said. "You tried."

And she really had, too. After she left, I felt like a bigger jerk than ever for using my great wardrobe to bribe her into trying to get my diary back. Even giving her the blue pants and top won't make up for what I wrote about her, I told myself. After Friday night, she'll hate me just like everybody else.

The trouble was, I had said things in that diary that no one would understand. I had meant them at the moment I wrote them because I was hurt or angry, but they weren't really the *truth*. Not the truth about the kids I wrote about, and now that I had stopped to think about it, not the truth about how I really felt.

Later, when I climbed into bed, I could almost hear the time bomb ticking. Wednesday. Thursday. Friday. Friday night. I was a goner. Blown away by my own diary. It was just a matter of time.

13 *

By morning I knew what I had to do.

I had tossed and turned all night thinking of my choices. The first choice was to skip the party and go to the audition the way I was supposed to. That would make my mother happy, and I might even get the job doing the commercial. But that wouldn't solve my problem. It was the second choice that made the most sense.

Skipping breakfast, I left for school a few minutes early. I wanted to get there in time to be the first one at the spot by the fence where The Fabulous Five always congregated in the morning. I planned to be there, waiting for them, when they arrived.

Jana and Melanie were the first to get to school. They came sauntering onto the playground as if they didn't have a care in the world. They didn't, I thought. Nobody had *their* diaries and was planning to expose their innermost secrets to the whole world.

They gave me a questioning look as they approached.

"Hi," I said nonchalantly, acting as if it were perfectly natural for me to be standing there.

"Hi," they said in unison. I knew that they were trying to figure out what to say next, but just then the other three girls came walking up.

"Hi, Taffy," said Christie. "Is something wrong?"

For an instant I lost my nerve as I looked at the five of them lined up like an army against me. If this didn't work, I was doomed worse than ever. Maybe I shouldn't even try it. Jana might see this as the perfect chance to get me for once and for all.

"Yeah," said Jana. "What's the matter?"

I hesitated, still trying to decide if I should take the chance. And yet, I couldn't help remembering when Jana and I had found baby Ashley. We had shared something so special that for a moment it felt as if we were friends. It had been confusing, and I had tried to explain it to my diary.

Dear Diary:

How can you hate someone and really like her at the same time? How can you suddenly feel like trusting someone who has been your enemy forever? That's what I'd like to know because it happened to me today.

First, Jana Morgan got me into trouble by saying that I stuck out my foot and tripped her—which I didn't do!!!!! Then, Miss Wiggins got mad at both of us for yelling at each other and sent us to the detention room in the office. Boy, was I mad. Then it happened. While we were walking in the hall, Jana thought she heard a kitten crying. We couldn't find it, and then I looked out the glass front doors and saw a baby in a basket. Her name was Ashley, and she had been abandoned right there on the steps of Mark Twain Elementary. Nobody else was around when we brought her into the hall. We talked to her and took care of her for a little while as if we were her mothers. We loved her so much! You could tell that she loved us, too, by the way she smiled.

When Jana and I looked at each other, it was as if we had the most wonderful secret in the world. It's hard to explain, but I wish that moment could have lasted forever.

Jana was still looking at me, waiting for me to answer. "I need to talk to you about my diary." I said the words quickly before I could chicken out again. "I know you have it and that you've read it. Even though you probably won't believe this, I just wanted to tell you that I'm sorry for all the mean things I wrote about you."

All five of them were staring at me as if I had just announced that school wouldn't be out for another six months. Jana started to say something, but I began talking again before she could get the words out.

"I don't know which one of you put the note on my desk with the drawing of the diary and the words 'Friday night' written on it, but I know what you're planning to do. You're going to read my diary out loud at the party and humiliate me in front of everybody. I promise, if you'll give it back to me *now*, I'll be your friend." I paused for an instant and looked at Jana, hoping that she would remember what it was like when we found baby Ashley.

Nobody said a word. I looked down at the ground as I waited, my heart pounding in my ears. I had said it. I had apologized to Jana and her friends. If this didn't work, I didn't know what else I could do.

Finally Jana spoke. "We don't have it, Taffy. Honest, we don't."

"That's right," said Beth. "All we found was that dirty magazine. We only pretended that we might have your diary."

"Are you sure someone's planning to read it at the party?" asked Jana. "That's awful."

I opened my purse and pulled out the crumpled note and handed it to her. "And look. It says 'Friday night,' just as I told you it did. What else could it mean?"

The girls passed it around, studying it closely and shaking their heads.

"Wow," said Melanie. "That's pretty scary. Somebody's definitely out to get you."

"But who?" said Katie.

We scanned the playground looking for anyone who might be suspicious, but none of us came up with any ideas.

I can't explain how, but I knew that Jana and her friends were telling the truth. They didn't have my diary after all. I walked around Mark Twain Elementary like a zombie all day, going to class, having lunch in the cafeteria, and feeling more depressed than ever. It was Thursday—the day before the party—and not only did I still not have my diary back, but I didn't even know who had it.

Most kids were bubbling over with excitement over leaving grade school and going into junior high in the fall. On the way home from school even Randy talked about how he could hardly wait for September and playing on the Wakeman football team, and he didn't seem to notice that I was quiet again.

As usual, my mother was waiting for me when I got in the house. She was in a dither, her face pink with excitement. I groaned under my breath. She was the last person I wanted to talk to right now.

"Oh, love, just wait until you hear the news," she gushed. "Cynthia Cameron will never be able to top this."

She paused, waiting breathlessly for me to ask her about her big news. When I didn't, she went on anyway.

"A little while ago I got this brilliant idea. You're going to be a star, and you should arrive at the television station like a star! So I rented a limousine to take you to the audition!"

I gasped. "A limousine?"

"That's right, dear. Tomorrow night, at exactly seven o'clock, an enormous white stretch limousine will pull up to our door. Then a uniformed chauffeur will escort you out to the car, put you inside, and take you to the audition in style. He'll wait, of course, and after you've given a stunning performance at the station, he'll drive you home again where your father and I will be waiting for you with bated breath."

I swallowed a giggle as what she was saying began to sink in.

"Then you and Dad aren't going with me?" I asked tentatively.

"Of course not, dear. How would it look for a *star* to arrive with her parents? But don't worry about a thing. You'll be wonderful."

Later, after I had thanked her a million times and was finally alone in my room, I hugged myself with joy. I had a new plan. A fantastic plan. It didn't matter that someone was going to try to humiliate me by reading my diary at the party. I would show that person a thing or two. I would show that person the *truth* about Taffy Sinclair!

14 ✿

Miss Wiggins had tears in her eyes as the final dismissal bell of the year rang the next afternoon. "It's been a wonderful year," she said. "Good luck in Wakeman Junior High. I'm going to miss you. Oh, yes," she added. "Every one of you has passed!"

A cheer went up when she said that. Naturally Clarence Marshall cheered the loudest. A lot of girls were crying when we filed out of the room. Not me. I couldn't have been happier. And neither could Curtis Trowbridge. He had been stopping kids in the halls all day reminding them about his party.

"Don't forget to be there at seven sharp. That's when it starts," he called out, "and we're going to have a big fire in the barbecue pit and roast wieners and make s'mores. It'll be great!"

I had smiled to myself when he stopped me at morning recess to give me his message. I had been on my way to the office to make a phone call. Mrs. Lockwood, the school secretary, let me use the phone after I assured her that it was a local call. Then I took the phone number of the television station out of my purse, dialed, and listened nervously to it ring.

When the station's receptionist answered, I took a deep breath and said, "May I speak to the casting director, please?"

"Who is calling?"

"This is Taffy Sinclair. I have an appointment for an audition this evening."

"One moment, Miss Sinclair."

I shifted from one foot to the other as I waited. Finally a man's voice said, "McDougal here. What can I do for you, Miss Sinclair? You are still planning to audition for us, aren't you?"

"Oh, yes," I said quickly. Then I faked a couple of coughs and went on, "But I have a little cold today, and my eyes are red." I coughed a few more times. "I was wondering if it might be better to postpone the audition until in the morning. I'm sure I'll be perfectly fine after a good night's rest."

Mr. McDougal didn't say anything for a moment. I tried not to panic. If he said no, it would blow all my big plans.

"Sure," he said pleasantly. "I was just checking my schedule, and I have an open slot at nine in the morning. How does that sound?"

"Terrific, Mr. McDougal. Thanks a million. I'll see you in the morning at nine."

"Good. And, Miss Sinclair . . ."

"Yes?" I asked nervously.

"I hope your cough is better in the morning."

"Oh! *Thanks!*" Then I coughed again for his benefit and hung up.

Next I dialed the limousine company. I had sneaked a look at my mother's bulletin board by the kitchen phone to get the number.

"Executive Limousine. May I help you?"

I crossed my fingers behind my back. "Certainly," I said in my most grown-up voice. "This is Mrs. Sinclair. I have a limousine reserved for this evening to take my daughter to the television studio for an audition."

"Yes, Mrs. Sinclair. We have your reservation right here. Is anything wrong?"

"Oh, heavens, no. I would just like to change the destination this evening and reserve another limo to take her to the television station in the morning instead. She's in such demand that I can hardly keep up with her schedule."

The lady at the limousine company must have believed that I was my mother because she made the changes I asked for in the reservation. Everything was set. I would take the limousine to the party tonight, and then, when I got home, I would tell my parents that the station wanted to do a second audition in the morning and that I had already informed the limo driver that he should pick me up at eight-thirty. Since my mother had said that a star never arrived with her parents, they would never know the difference.

The first thing I did when I got home from school was take my new sundress out of the closet and spread it across my bed. It was even prettier than I remembered with all the bright colors splashing through it, and it made me feel good to look at it. I could hardly wait to put it on. It would be perfect for the party tonight.

Mother came into my room after I had showered and dressed. She was all excited and had her arms loaded. "I brought my makeup and some other things," she said. "After all, if you're going to be on television, you need a little eye shadow to emphasize your beautiful blue eyes and some color for your cheeks and lips."

I was too excited to trust my voice, so I only nodded and let her tie a towel around my neck the way the makeup lady had done on the set of *Interns and Lovers*. Things were working out too terrifically to be true.

Finally, seven o'clock came. As I stood by the window in my beautiful new dress watching for the limousine, I thought about all the kids from my class arriving at Curtis Trowbridge's house for the party at this very moment. They would all be there. Jana Morgan would probably be dropped off by her mother and her mother's friend, Pink. Jana's friends and Alexis and Scott and Keith and, of course, Randy Kirwan would come in their family cars.

Just then a sleek white limousine pulled up at the curb. It was the longest car I had ever seen and the most beautiful. It had six doors along each side, and the windows were tinted so that you couldn't see who was inside. A tall, thin chauffeur in a dark suit and a hat with a visor stepped out and came to the door, bowing stiffly when I opened it and saying, "Miss Sinclair? I'm here to drive you."

After my parents had both hugged me and wished me luck a jillion times, I took a deep breath and followed him out to the car. When he held one of the doors open for me, I hesitated an instant. Maybe I was making a mistake, I thought wildly. Maybe it wouldn't work.

But hadn't my mother always told me to hold my head high and ignore what people were saying about me? I got into the car, and we drove away.

15 ✳

I could see the fire in Curtis's barbecue pit as soon as the limousine rounded the corner onto his street. It was almost dark, and through the tinted windows the kids scampering around the yard looked like demons in the glow of the firelight.

"I'll be back for you at nine o'clock, Miss," the chauffeur said when the car came to a stop in front of Curtis's house. I nodded. Then I allowed him to open the door for me, and I stepped out.

Every single person in Curtis's yard had stopped and was looking at me with admiration. I was Cinderella getting out of her carriage. I was the Queen of England. I was a movie star arriving at the

105

Academy Awards. I was Madonna stepping out on stage. I raised my head high, squared my shoulders, and walked through the gate to join the party. I would die before I'd let anyone know how much I was hurting inside.

At first no one said a word. They just stood there in the shimmering firelight and stared at me.

Finally, Mona rushed forward and grabbed my hand. "Come on, Taffy. You're the last one here, and we're having fun!"

I blinked and gave Mona a second look. She was wearing the blue outfit I had given her, and she really looked gorgeous. She giggled when she saw the expression on my face, and I started to compliment her when Curtis raced up to me.

"Gosh, Taffy. That was some entrance. Where'd you get that limo?"

I had made up my mind to be mysterious about the limousine, so I ignored his question. "It looks like a great party, Curtis," I said. "I'm sorry I'm late. Oh, by the way. Is it true that your parents aren't home?"

Curtis looked embarrassed. "You must be the tenth person who has asked me that. I don't know who started that rumor. They're here, all right, but they promised to stay in the house."

A moment later Curtis was off and running again, passing out pointed sticks. A table was set near the barbecue pit, and it was piled high with wieners, buns, mustard, ketchup, and potato chips. Soft drinks were cooling in a tub of ice nearby.

Everyone seemed to be having a wonderful time, but suddenly as I stood there alone, my old fear came back to me. Someone here at this very party had my diary, and whoever it was, was planning to read it out loud. I shivered even though it was a warm night and looked around. Over to one side of the yard Mona was talking to Matt Zeboski. Were they holding hands? It was too shadowy to tell for sure. I giggled and looked away. Jana and her friends were talking to Keith Masterson and Joel Murphy, and Randy and Scott Daly were holding twigs over the barbecue pit until they caught fire and then pretending that they were smoking them. Those fakes, I thought and smiled.

Clarence Marshall had already started roasting wieners. In fact, he had threaded three onto his stick, and they were so heavy that the stick snapped and they fell sizzling into the fire.

"Rats!" he shouted, and looked around for another stick. Just then he spotted me. "Hey, Taffy," he shouted. "Don't forget that you owe me a kiss."

"That jerk," I muttered. "He'd better leave me alone." Lisa Snow and Kim Baxter were starting a game of badminton under the light from the porch, and I hurried in their direction.

"Can I play?" I asked.

"Sure. Here, catch."

Lisa tossed me a racket, and we batted the birdie around until Kim announced that she was too hungry to play anymore.

"Me, too," I admitted, and the three of us headed for the fire.

I was beginning to relax. It was almost eight o'clock and nothing had happened. Maybe the person who had my diary had had a change of heart. Maybe whoever that person was had seen me arrive in the big white limousine and had decided that it was impossible to hurt me. I hoped so. That would mean that my plan had worked.

Just then Randy Kirwan stepped up beside me. "It's a great party, isn't it?"

I nodded, and then I started to laugh.

"What's so funny?" he asked.

"I was just remembering that at school earlier this week some of the girls were wondering if we'd have to work crossword puzzles or play computer games when we came to Curtis's house."

"Curtis is okay," said Randy. "He's just misunderstood."

I was aching to turn to Randy and say, *So am I*, but I didn't.

Lisa and Kim and I roasted hot dogs and ate them and were standing around talking when Curtis called from the center of the yard, "Come on, everybody. It's dark enough to play hide-and-seek tag. Okay, who wants to be It?"

"Me!" shouted Richie Corrierro.

He covered his eyes and started counting while everybody scrambled to hide. I squeezed behind the back wall of the house and a bush and held my breath.

"Ready or not, here I come," called Richie.

Richie went streaking around the yard catching Alexis and Eric Silverman while Randy and Mark and Jana ran home free.

Richie was moving steadily toward the part of the yard where I was hiding. He had already caught Melanie and Christie, and I had a feeling I would be next. I eased my way out from behind the bush and ducked around the side of the house. It was totally dark. He would never find me here.

Almost everyone else had either been caught or had made it home free, and I edged toward the corner of the house to peek. Just then someone tapped me on the shoulder. I looked up into Clarence Marshall's grinning face.

"What's the matter? Did I scare you?"

I narrowed my eyes and scowled at him. "Of course not. I'm not scared of you."

"Then give me that kiss you owe me."

"I don't owe you any kiss," I insisted. "Now leave me alone."

"Sure. Whatever you say." He started to back away, but when he did, he stepped into the light and I got a flash of something blue that he was waving in his hand. My diary! "But if you want this back, you'd better give me a kiss."

I stood there staring at him for an instant before pandemonium broke loose. Kids came from every direction, and Clarence went down like a quarterback being sacked in the middle of a pass. I started to grab for my diary, but before I could move, someone else wrenched it out of his hand.

It was Jana, and she tucked it under her arm as she got to her feet. My heart stopped. What was she going to do? Slowly everyone else untangled themselves from the pile of bodies and stood up, too, and I realized for the first time that it had been The Fabulous Five who had tackled Clarence.

"Jeez," he said, sitting up and rubbing a spot on his head. "Knocked down by a bunch of girls! I wasn't going to do anything! Honest! I was just having a little fun."

"We didn't like your idea of fun," said Jana. "And what's more, this diary is private property. It belongs to Taffy Sinclair."

Then Jana stepped over Clarence's outstretched legs and held the diary out to me. "Here's your diary back. Now we know who had it and why. He wasn't going to read it tonight. He was just going to bribe you into giving him a kiss."

"Thanks," I whispered as my chin started to quiver. I had never been so grateful to anyone in my entire life. "Thanks a million."

I took my diary, thinking that I was beginning to feel differently about Jana and her friends, and from the way they had ganged up on Clarence, I suspected that they felt differently about me, too. Not that we could ever be best friends, I reasoned. Too much had happened between us for that. But maybe we wouldn't be enemies when we got to Wakeman Junior High, either. Maybe the truth about all of us was that we were too grown up for that sort of thing anymore. Maybe I was too grown up for a diary, too, I thought. Then, with everyone watching, I tossed it into the fire.

16 ❋

*A*fter that, no one wanted to play hide-and-seek tag anymore, so we went into Curtis's house to listen to music.

"Can you believe that nerdy old Curtis has a compact disk player and all the best music?" whispered Alexis.

"He's not as nerdy as you think," I whispered back. "He's just misunderstood."

The rest of the party was pretty mellow. Clarence sat in a corner by himself and pouted. Every so often I could hear him grumbling about how having my diary had all just been a big joke. Everyone else sprawled on toss pillows on the family room floor, drinking sodas and listening to music. Finally it was almost nine o'clock and kids got ready to leave.

I glanced across the room at Randy as I stood up and smoothed the wrinkles out of my beautiful new sundress. He was the only part of my plan that hadn't worked out. I had dreamed of us finding a dark corner and being alone, maybe even kissing good-night when the party was over.

What's the use? I thought. After all, he's Jana's boyfriend, and she was the one who saved me from terrible humiliation tonight.

I looked at Randy again, thinking that he was the handsomest boy in our class. There probably wouldn't be anyone else nearly as handsome in Wakeman next year.

Suddenly something occurred to me. Something fantastic. In fact, it was all I could do to keep from jumping all over the place and laughing out loud. True, Randy hadn't spent much time with me tonight, but he also hadn't spent much time with Jana, either. That had to mean I still had a chance with him after all!

My limousine would be here for me any minute. I wondered if Randy had ever ridden in a car like that. I could offer him a ride home. Of course we'd be alone—behind the tinted windows. I hesitated a moment. I honestly didn't want to hurt Jana now that we weren't total enemies, but wasn't my mother's favorite old saying something about everything's being fair in *love* and war?

I smiled to myself and headed across the room.

"Randy," I called in my sweetest voice. "Can I talk to you a minute?"

"Sure." He was looking straight at me and giving me a fabulous smile.

I hurried toward him, suddenly remembering everything I had ever known about making conversation with cute boys. "I was wondering if you'd like a ride home in my limo?" I asked. At the same time I opened my eyes as wide as I could so that he would notice how blue they were and flipped my long blond hair over my shoulder. "It's such a BIG car for one person. I'd really like it if you came along to keep me company."

"Wow! Do you mean it?" he asked excitedly. "I'd love to ride in a humongous car like that." He was grinning so big that I knew he really meant it, so I wasn't prepared for what he said next.

"I've got an even better idea. You've got so much room, why don't you give EVERYBODY a ride home?"

A cheer went up, and kids started jumping around, laughing and giggling and crowding toward the front door.

"Terrific."

"Thanks, Taffy."

"A limousine! I can't believe it!"

It was pandemonium. Some kids lined up at the phone to call their parents and tell them not to pick them up. Others were shouting their appreciation to me for the chance to ride in a limousine, and a few even shook my hand and acted as if I were their long-lost friend. Only Clarence hung back, looking embarrassed as the chauffeur began opening car doors and letting kids pile in.

I sighed. Boy, some days nothing turned out the way you expected it to, I thought. Jana didn't have my diary. Clarence did. And Randy accepted my invitation to ride home and then invited the rest of the world. Now the entire sixth—whoops!—*seventh*-grade class thought I was wonderful. I glanced back at Clarence. If this was what making friends was all about, I couldn't just leave him standing there.

"Come on, Clarence," I called. "You can ride, too."

I stuffed myself into the middle row of seats between Marcie Bee and Joel Murphy, listening to the happy murmuring of my friends and thinking that I would probably even break down and confess to my parents that I had gone to the party tonight instead of the audition. I had the feeling that now I could make them understand. In fact, I was feeling so happy and so confident that I knew I would get the TV job. Cynthia Cameron didn't stand a chance.

Suddenly as we pulled away from the curb, someone from the seat behind poked me on the shoulder. "You know what, Taffy?" Clarence boomed, and when I turned around to look at him, he was grinning from ear to ear. "The truth is, you're not such a bad kid after all."

Good news from Bantam Skylark Books! The five best friends who formed the Against Taffy Sinclair Club now have a series of their own. It's new. It's fun. It's fabulous. It's The Fabulous Five!

Read on for more exciting details.

MEET THE
FABULOUS FIVE!

Jana Morgan, Katie Shannon, Christie Winchell, Beth Barry, and Melanie Edwards have been best friends ever since they first met in Mark Twain Elementary School. The Fabulous Five have always stuck together, especially when that meant keeping up with their archrival Taffy Sinclair—the most beautiful and stuck-up girl in school. Now The Fabulous Five are leaving sixth grade and moving on up to Wakeman Junior High School. In a new school the girls will especially need to stick together, especially when they meet up with a group of girls who call themselves The Fantastic Foursome.

JANA MORGAN

Full of terrific ideas and loyal to the core, Jana Morgan helps keep The Fabulous Five together through thick and thin. Although she has tons of friends and the cutest boy from Mark Twain Elementary as her boyfriend, Jana sometimes doubts herself, and this can get her into sticky situations.

BETH BARRY

With her brightly colored clothes and dramatic flourishes, Beth Barry has always been a bit of a class clown. Sometimes she gets carried away with her silly antics, but her friends agree that she's always fun to have around.

MELANIE EDWARDS

Melanie Edwards used to be overweight from eating too many of her mom's homemade brownies, but now she's very thin. Melanie is always insisting to her friends that she's not boy crazy, but even she has to admit that she *loves* to flirt.

CHRISTIE WINCHELL

The daughter of the principal at Mark Twain Elementary School, Christie Winchell has always felt at home there. Now that she has graduated to seventh grade, she's a little nervous about a new school and all of the schoolwork, but she's a total whiz at math and ready to help her friends through any crisis.

KATIE SHANNON

Red-haired Katie Shannon is a pint-sized feminist who has picked up her mom's campaign for women's rights. Outspoken Katie is always telling her friends about how women are degraded and is always urging them to fight for this cause.

MEET THE FANTASTIC FOURSOME!

Laura McCall, Funny Hawthorne, Tammy Lucero, and Melissa McConnell are four best friends who call themselves The Fantastic Foursome. They were the most popular girls at Riverfield Elementary, and they're determined to fit into Wakeman Junior High in the same way—even if it means competing with The Fabulous Five!

LAURA MCCALL

The leader of The Fantastic Foursome, Laura McCall is *very* pretty and *very* bossy. Because of her bossiness she's sometimes called "the witch" behind her back. But Laura can surprise even those who know her best with her sweetness and loyalty.

"FUNNY" HAWTHORNE

Nicknamed "Funny" for her bright personality, Karin Janelle Hawthorne is the kind of person who can always cheer you up. She's sometimes called a "bubblehead" by the kids who don't know her well, but everyone loves to have her around.

TAMMY LUCERO

Tammy Lucero can't help it—she loves to gossip! Even her best friends know not to —ell her their deepest secrets. Tammy sometimes tells things she shouldn't by accident, and even though she means no harm, not everybody understands.

MELISSA MCCONNELL

Melissa McConnell is a perfectionist with a capital "P". Her family tells her she's too hard on herself, and her friends tease her about being perfect all the time. Melissa tries to relax a little, but she doesn't always succeed.

And here are some of the other characters you'll be reading about in the new The Fabulous Five series:

SHANE ARRINGTON

Most kids see Shane Arrington as the coolest guy around. He has a pet iguana, and nothing ever gets to him! And all of the girls agree that he looks absolutely gorgeous in his football uniform.

WHITNEY LARKIN

Whitney Larkin is supposed to be in sixth grade, but she's so brilliant that she has skipped right up to seventh. A lot of kids are uncomfortable around her because they're afraid they'll say something dumb. What they don't know is that having a high IQ can often be the loneliest thing in the world.

JON SMITH

Jon Smith sees himself as the most boring person alive. Even his name is plain! Jon sometimes has trouble seeing his good points, mostly because he's trying to live up to his parents, local TV personalities.

Here are some excerpts from The Fabulous Five #1, *Seventh-Grade Rumors.*

"Oh, my gosh!" shrieked Beth. "*Look!* They're standing in our spot!"

Jana and her friends had just entered the gates of Wakeman Junior High on Tuesday morning and were making their way across the crowded school ground toward the front left corner of the fence just as they had planned. At Beth's outburst they stopped and looked with surprise in the direction she was pointing.

"Oh, no!" cried Jana. It was true. Four girls were standing in the very spot The Fabulous Five had picked as their own on Saturday, looking as if the world belonged to them. One was a tall blonde whose hair had been caught on top of her head and fell over one shoulder in a braid that came almost to her waist. Beside her stood her exact opposite, a small dark-haired girl who had a short haircut and enormous brown eyes. Next to her was another blonde, and beside her a wide-eyed brunette with long, wavy hair. It was obvious who was in control—the tall blonde with the waist-length braid. The moment she spoke the other three turned toward her with the precision of a drill team and seemed to hang on her every word.

"Laura McCall," Melanie muttered. "I know it's her. It has to be. And those are the rest of The Fantastic Foursome."

"What are *they* doing in our place?" Beth demanded. "Come on. Let's get them out of there."

"How?" asked Christie. "This is a public school. They have as much right to be there as we do."

Beth didn't seem to hear. She was heading straight toward the other girls with determination written on her face.

"Beth!" insisted Jana, running after her best friend. "Wait. We can't just go barreling up to them and tell them to get out of our private spot. After all, Christie's right. This is a public school."

"Whatever we do, we have to stick together," said Melanie.

"Yeah," said Katie. "Remember that we're The Fabulous Five." Then she paused, throwing an angry look toward Laura McCall and her followers. "The Fantastic Foursome," she scoffed. "Big deal."

By now it was obvious to Jana that The Fantastic Foursome had noticed The Fabulous Five and were glaring back at them.

"I don't like this," said Melanie in a voice that was almost a whimper. "Let's get out of here."

"Don't be ridiculous," barked Beth. "They're not going to scare me off."

Katie moved up to stand beside Beth. "Me either," she said.

At the same instant, Laura McCall stepped forward. "What do you want?" she challenged.

"Did you *lose* something?" asked the short, dark-haired girl beside her.

"Of course not," Beth threw back at her. "We just wanted to look you over since we've heard so much about you."

Laura McCall froze instantly. Her eyes hardened as she looked straight at Beth. "You must be Beth Barry. We've heard all about you, too."

The three girls standing beside Laura giggled. "You're the show-off," Laura assured her.

Jana felt a burst of anger at Laura for saying such a thing. Beth was dressed in chartreuse stirrup pants and a chartreuse and electric-pink shirt that hung past her knees. She had wild taste in clothes, but that didn't make her a show-off. She was just a little theatrical, that was all. Also, what had Laura meant when she told Beth that they had heard all about her? Was someone spreading rumors? Telling lies? If so, maybe not just about Beth. Maybe those lies extended to herself and the rest of her friends. After all, Laura hadn't said *you're A show-off*. She had said *you're THE show-off*, as if she had more labels that she was just waiting to slap onto other kids whenever she felt like it. I wonder what my label is? The what?

Turning into the left corridor, Jana and Christie hurried along, scanning the first few room numbers looking for 107, their homeroom. Suddenly Christie stopped short and reached out a hand to halt Jana.

Looking up, Jana saw that five or six boys, probably ninth graders, were lined up in the hall. They were watching the two approach with amused smiles on their faces.

"Hey, guys, look what we have here," one of them said. "Seventh-grade girls. What do you think?"

"Ignore them and just keep walking," Christie whispered hoarsely. "Act natural."

Jana tried, but her legs felt instantly stiff. Her knees didn't want to bend and her feet shuffled noisily across the floor.

"I'd say they're threes," called a boy from the far end of the line. "Three and a half, tops."

"Naw, three is too generous."

Jana cringed. Suddenly she knew what was going on. The boys were ninth graders looking over the new crop of seventh-grade girls, and they were stationed along the hallway to rate—probably on a scale of one to ten—any seventh-grade girls unlucky enough to come by.

Three is too generous! she thought angrily. Of all the nerve. But then, who cared what a few ninth-grade boys thought, anyway? The important thing was to get out of there and find the right room before the bell rang.

Suddenly the boys started hooting and clapping. "Ten! Ten!" someone shouted.

Surprised, Jana turned around to see Laura McCall sauntering up the hall with her long blonde braid bouncing over her shoulder and a triumphant gleam in her eye.

Here is a scene from Book #2, *The Trouble With Flirting.*

"I am not boy crazy!" Melanie insisted. A hurt expression crossed her face as she sank back into the booth at Bumpers, the fast-food restaurant decorated with bumper cars from an old amusement park ride that was the junior high hangout. She scanned her four best friends' faces for signs of sympathy.

"Hey, look," said Katie. "Here comes Scott Daly, and he's with Shane Arrington. "What do you suppose they're talking about?"

Melanie's eyes brightened and she spun around, looking hopefully toward the front door where kids were streaming in for after-school sodas. Her shoulders slumped the instant she realized that Katie had only been teasing her, pretending that the two boys she had mad crushes on were coming into Bumpers together. Still, she knew her friends loved to tease her about her interest in boys.

"Listen, you guys," she said, laughing. "I just happen to like boys, that's all. What's so unusual about that?"

Jana leaned toward Melanie, her smile fading. "Speaking of boys, have you heard any more about Laura McCall's party?"

"No," said Melanie with a frown. "All I know is that Laura and The Fantastic Foursome are passing out invitations in *red envelopes*, and that every single seventh-grade boy who went to Mark Twain Elementary has gotten one—including Scott Daly. And even worse, they are all planning to go."

"What a dirty trick," said Christie. "A real bummer."

"It just means that she's afraid of the competition," Katie said smugly.

"Yeah," agreed Beth. "She knows that if The Fabulous Five were there, she'd never stand a chance."

Melanie didn't answer. She was too worried. Everyone knew that Laura had a crush on Shane Arrington, the gorgeous hunk from her own school, and that she had parties just so she could invite him. Shane could win a River Phoenix look-alike contest hands down, but there were other things about him that were special, too. He had parents who were hippies and a pet iguana named Igor. Melanie had never met anyone like him before. For Laura to go after Shane was bad enough, now that Melanie liked him, too, in addition to still liking her old boyfriend, Scott Daly. But for Laura to invite the Mark Twain boys to this party meant that she would have the perfect opportunity to go after *both* Shane and Scott at once without any interference from The Fabulous Five. The idea made Melanie's reddish-brown hair curl.

"I can't believe that Randy Kirwan will go," said Jana in a sad voice. "Not after all he and I have meant to each other."

Beth nodded. "Or Keith Masterson, either."

"Well, if Scott goes, Laura had better keep her hands off him," Melanie declared.

"So, what are you going to do if she doesn't?" asked Katie.

"I don't know, but I'll think of something."

Watch for one book each month in The Fabulous Five series, starting in August!

ABOUT THE AUTHOR

In addition to The Fabulous Five series, Betsy Haynes is the author of the Taffy Sinclair series, and the books *The Great Mom Swap* and *The Great Boyfriend Trap,* all available from Bantam Skylark Books. Mrs. Haynes enjoys writing about the girls in The Fabulous Five and uses her lap computer to tell their stories. The author lives in Colleyville, Texas.

THE CLASS TRIP

SWEET VALLEY TWINS SUPER EDITION #1

Join Jessica and Elizabeth in the very first SWEET VALLEY TWINS Super Edition—it's longer, can be read out of sequence, and is full of page-turning excitement!

The day of the big sixth-grade class trip to the Enchanted Forest is finally here! But Jessica and Elizabeth have a fight and spend the beginning of the trip arguing. When Elizabeth decides to make up, Jessica has disappeared. In a frantic search for her sister, Elizabeth finds herself in a series of dangerous and exciting Alice In Wonderland-type of adventures.

☐ 15588-1 $2.95/$3.50 in Canada

Buy them at your local bookstore or use this page to order.

- -

Skylark is Riding High with Books for Girls Who Love Horses!

☐ **A HORSE OF HER OWN by Joanna Campbell**
15564-4 $2.75 ($3.25 in Canada)
Like many 13-year-olds, Penny Rodgers has always longed to ride a horse. Since her parents won't pay for lessons, Penny decides to try her hand at training an old horse named Bones. When she turns him into a champion jumper, Penny proves to everyone that she's serious about riding!

☐ **RIDING HOME by Pamela Dryden**
15591-1 $2.50 ($2.95 in Canada)
Betsy Lawrence has loved horses all her life, and until her father's remarriage, was going to get her own horse! But now there's just not enough money. And Betsy can't help resenting her new stepsister Ferris, who is pretty, neat, does well in school, and gets all the music lessons she wants—Ferris loves music the way Betsy loves horses. Can the two girls ever learn to be sisters—and even friends?

New Series!

☐ **HORSE CRAZY: THE SADDLE CLUB: BOOK #1 by B.B. Hiller**
15594-6 $2.95 ($3.50 in Canada)
Beginning with HORSE CRAZY: BOOK #1, this four-book miniseries tells the stories of three very different girls with one thing in common: horses! Fun-loving Stevie and serious Carole are at Pine Hollow Stables for their usual lesson, when they meet another 12-year-old named Lisa. Her elaborate riding outfit prompts the girls to play a practical joke on her. After Lisa retaliates a truce is formed, and so is THE SADDLE CLUB!
Look for HORSE SHY: BOOK #2, Coming in July 1988!

- -